THIS RANGE IS MINE

Sam Allee's half-brother Drake hounded him out of Wyoming's rich North Park country. But Sam fought back, bought his own ranch and hired a gang of killers to defend his land against Drake's greed.

But there was greed both ways. Drake wanted Sam's land, but Sam hungered for Drake's woman. And the hired killers were itching for action. The feud had to end in violence, gunsmoke and death for one brother or the other; and Sam held one joker, secretly, to make sure it wasn't for him.

THIS RANGE IS MINE

John Hunter

GUNSMOKE

First published in the UK by Hale

This hardback edition 2008
by BBC Audiobooks Ltd
by arrangement with
Golden West Literary Agency

ISBN 978 1 405 68179 7

British Library Cataloguing in Publication Data available.

Printed and bound in Great Britain by
Antony Rowe Ltd., Chippenham, Wiltshire

1

In the ten hours since the rocking, jolting stage had left the Express at the new station of Laramie, Sam Allee had tried not to be caught studying the girl on the opposite seat. He had been looking at her ever since she came aboard the train at Council Bluffs for the long trip westward, and he had blessed his lucky star when she too changed to the southbound stagecoach. He and she had been the only passengers to leave the railroad at Laramie, and now they were the only travelers on the stage.

To Sam's mind she was well worth studying: a little above average height, a neatly put together figure in a soft-brown traveling dress. Her face was a trifle long for classic beauty, but there was an attractive proud poise to the way she sat. Her hair was soft gold where a ringlet escaped beneath the edge of her bonnet. And the bonnet ribbons were tied in a bow under her chin, the long ends falling to her waist, the whole a beguiling frame for her ivory features. Her coloring told Sam she was not of this part of the country. No matter what care ranch women took with their complexions, the exposure to wind and sun dried their skins to the look of cordovan leather.

He had no idea who she was. She held herself aloof, and he had not tried to speak with her as other men would have done. She wore no rings.

"I am going," he told himself, "to learn where she's headed. I am going to marry her."

It was an idea that had been working its way to

1

the front of his mind throughout the trip, crowding through the harsher plans he knew he would soon be involved with. It was the first time Sam Allee had entertained the thought of marriage, and the decision that had just ripened—to marry a girl without knowing even her name—struck him as so absurd he involuntarily laughed aloud.

She had been gazing through the side window at the timber they were running through as through a tunnel. The coach had bridged the Laramie at Woods Crossing and was climbing the stiff grade toward the plateau at the top of the ridge, beyond which lay the long drop into the valley of the Canadian.

At his laugh her head came around and she said in surprise, "What's so funny?" The moment the words were spoken she bit her lip and her face colored. "I . . . I am sorry. I didn't mean to be rude. It just slipped out."

Allee was embarrassed for her. With a quick smile of reassurance he told her, "I'm glad of it. For the past seven days I've been trying to work up the courage to speak. What made me laugh? Just a stray thought that hit me."

She withdrew again, went back to watching the trees and the occasional camp where men lived who cut ties for the transcontinental railroad. Allee wanted to continue the talk, but he did not know how to start it again, if indeed it had really started at all.

They crossed the plateau in silence. The trail turned down, dropping in steady loops, passing the rugged entrance to Kings Canyon out of which Pinkham Creek rushed wildly to join its waters with the Canadian below. The stage careened around the turn and went on the two miles further to Cowdry post office. There squatted a single store built of squared logs. The driver wheeled up before it, calling down from the high box, "Half hour for dinner, folks."

The sun overhead made the coach interior sweltering. The girl who had been so cool and fresh at Laramie now was flushed by the heat a line of moist beads standing on her upper lip. She touched her lip with a frilly handkerchief and appealed to Sam Allee. "Is it safe to drink the water here?"

"Safe, and the sweetest anywhere," he assured her.

The thoroughbraces creaked loudly as he rose from the seat, bending double to keep his head from banging the roof. He opened the door, dropped to the ground without using the step, settled his wide hat and turned to offer her his hand. She hesitated, looked down at the dusty road and held out her small, gloved fingers. At the Laramie station there had been a footstool to help her mount the coach but there was no such amenity here. She lowered one foot to the narrow step, but the tight hem of her skirt would not let the other foot reach the ground unless she lifted her skirt to her knees. She would have to jump, and to judge by her expression, the idea did not appeal. Without a word Sam Allee took her elbows, swung her out and down. In his big arms she weighed nothing. He steadied her until she had her balance. Then, because touching her had made his pulse pound, he pivoted away and went with long strides up to the porch, opened the screen-door and held it for her. The screen was an affectation, keeping more buzzing flies inside than it kept out.

The small, low-ceilinged dining room was as hot as the coach, close with the smells of previous diners and the reek of grease. Two men were already eating, using their forks to shovel food onto their knives. Dust clinging to their eyebrows and stubble beards identified them to Sam as riders. They stopped, knives halfway to their mouths, to stare at the girl, caught Sam Allee's hard eyes on them, and dropped their attention again to the heaps of steak and beans on their plates.

The girl looked through them, passed with her chin high, and sat down at a table in the far corner, its top scrubbed white. The men's heads followed her and they mumbled low comments as Allee started toward the counter. He changed direction, went to the table and said quietly, "Would you object if I ate here too?"

She looked relieved, gave him a brief, tentative smile, and he folded into the opposite chair, tucking his boots under it where they would not touch her feet. For the first time she showed a frank interest in him. She saw a strong, well-knit man, almost a towhead above a sun-browned face, with a few freckles barely visible beneath the burn. It was the eyes that compelled her attention, an unusual gray-green flecked with gold, direct and devil-may-care. The mouth was well-defined and mobile, smiling now in a conspiracy to shield her from any approach by the riders. She sensed that this man could laugh and be dangerous at the same time, and her curiosity waked.

A stout woman in faded calico brought thick white plates filled with meat and beans, mugs of coffee, and tinny tableware. Putting them down, she mopped her face and neck, red from the stove, with her apron corner.

"There's dried apple pie later."

"Fine." Allee sounded enthusiastic, and when the woman had left, widened his smile on the girl. "By the way, I'm Sam Allee."

The girl started. "Oh? Would you be related to Drake Allee?"

"My half brother."

She sounded puzzled. "Strange I never heard him mention you."

"We don't talk much about each other. Never got along."

"Still, you'd think he would say something about

a brother. You see, I'm coming out here to marry him."

The smile blanked out of Sam's green eyes. His wide mouth tightened, giving his face a sudden cruel expression. It lasted less than a second until he got hold of himself, but in that instant the girl saw something there that frightened her. Then his easy smile was back and he said quietly, "Drake has a way of ignoring what he doesn't like. Where did you meet him?"

"In St. Louis. He'd been to Kansas City to sell beef, and a friend introduced us. Isn't he the handsome thing?"

Here it was again, all of it. Drake beating him out again. Drake had always been the handsomer, the stronger, their father's favorite. Sam was the one known for being in trouble often, not that he got *into* more trouble than Drake did, but Sam just had the knack of being caught.

As though she read his mind the girl asked, "Will you tell me what's wrong between you?"

His voice turned flat, empty. "Why don't you wait and let Drake explain? By the way, if you're going to be my new sister, shouldn't I know your name?"

She flushed, giving a strained, uncertain little laugh as though to ward off this man who was at odds with her fiancé, dropped her head, and cut intently at the tough meat with the dull knife.

"At the moment it's Martha Bollen."

That appeared to put an end to their getting further acquainted. He felt a wall rise between them and gave his attention to the food, almost vicious in his carving. Always Drake had gotten everything Sam wanted. Now apparently he would cheat him of this girl too.

When they returned to the coach Martha Bollen initiated a new conversation in apparent apology for her brusqueness in the restaurant.

"How much farther is it to Walden?"

"Ten or twelve miles." Sam sounded indifferent now.

The stage ran on with less jolt and sway, the road here nearly level at eight thousand feet above the sea, cutting through lush meadows where cattle grazed belly-deep in dark green grass. It was as fine a range as Sam had seen anywhere in his drifting across the West from Oregon through California and New Mexico and Texas. The reasons were not hard to find. The soil was deep, rich, the great Park drained by a dozen rivers and twice that many streams, a cattleman's heaven barring one misery, the bitter winters. It was not unheard of for a winter kill to wipe out half a herd, common to feed in temperatures far below zero. That separated the men from the boys.

The girl spoke again. "What lovely meadow."

Sam smiled, his sour mood lifting at the words, the tone of admiration. He remembered how his father had prayed before every meal that nothing would happen to the good grass.

"The big stuff is bluestem. Most of the Park has never been plowed, so you can still find some buffalo. It's a tough plant, but it spreads in clusters of runners, and once they've been plowed it's very hard to get them started again."

"I think that's a shame."

"A crime." He sounded bitter. "The greedy land agents are to blame, with their notion of colonizing the country with farmers. This land is good for only one thing, herding. Doesn't matter what kind of animals you run. Buffalo filled the place until the hide hunters wiped them out, and cattle do fine as long as you have the right place to feed them and feed enough to last the winter."

Her interest appeared genuine as she kept questioning. "What are they fed?"

"Hay, mostly."

"Timothy?"

Sam Allee was warming again, talking on his favorite subject. "No, that's eastern grass, from the Carolinas originally. Here it's bunch grass, well-cured. The stockmen swear by it."

"And you're a stockman?"

"Not yet. The last five years I've been wandering around the West learning and looking for a place to light and start."

"Did you find what you wanted?"

"Right back here in North Park. I am coming home."

"You'll buy a ranch?"

"I already have." He could not conceal the bleak note in his tone. "A place my brother ran a man named Allen off of and grabbed for himself."

Again she felt the chilling force within him and drew back into herself. She turned her eyes out of the window wondering what was ahead in her new life here, wondering if Sam Allee were telling the truth about Drake's high-handed treatment of the man Allen or if there weren't another side to the story. She did not speak again until they reached the town.

Walden was a disappointment, the business district centered on just one street. The only building of any size was the courthouse, standing apart on a bluff overlooking the scraggly community, a square box that was the pride of the county officers. All of it was dishearteningly drab in her eyes.

The stage stopped finally before the only hotel, a two-story unpainted wooden structure, the siding boards weather-stained and warping. The driver looped his lines, swung down, went to the back, and opened the rear boot, while Sam again lifted the girl out and set her on the wooden sidewalk. Allee turned to catch the bedroll that the driver tossed him. Then the girl's two traveling cases and bell-topped trunk were brought and set beside her.

Sam heaved the bedroll onto his shoulder, telling

the driver, "Put the trunk on the porch until Miss Bollen says what she wants done with it."

The girl stood looking helplessly around the dreary street. In front of the saloon across from the hotel, the boardwalk was filled with sitting men come to town for Saturday. It was a ritual throughout the West, and the Park was no exception. They had squatted, leaned, sat there since seven o'clock in the morning, hardly moving, seldom talking. Their eyes, sheltered under the wide hat-brims, were cool, direct, unblinking, surveying their small world.

Sam Allee knew them, their inner thoughts, their minor frustrations, their curiosities. He knew none of these by name nor what outfits they rode for, but he had seen a thousand of their brotherhood from Bend, Oregon, to San Antone.

He shifted the bedroll as it tried to slip, then nodded toward the hotel, asking the girl, "Do you want to register?"

She looked up, uncertain, her shoulders stiff. Sam saw that she was aware of the cowboys staring at her and resented it.

"Who are they? What are they doing?"

"Riders."

"Why aren't they riding?"

"It's Saturday." He explained that this was about the only holiday they ever had and saw her sniff.

"But there must be something for them to do beside just sit and gape."

Smiling at her reaction, he shrugged. "Oh, every half hour or so some of them go into the saloon, drink a beer, or shoot a game of pool on the table in the back. Shall I take your bags in here?"

"I don't know. Drake was to meet me or send someone, but he isn't here. I can't just stand on this walk with those men looking as if they'd never seen another woman."

"They probably never did see one like you. Come on in the lobby."

They had turned toward the door when a clatter drew their attention to the bottom of the street. A buckboard flung around the corner and raced toward them, the matched bays full out ahead of three riders bringing a saddled black.

Sam stopped the girl. "Here they come now."

Even at that distance Sam recognized the old mud wagon with the sides built up higher than normal. He set down the cases and faced the street, stepping apart from the girl. The driver hauled up close to the raised sidewalk, sat a long moment looking from one to the other while the riders came abreast. The nearest man dismounted. Then the driver anchored his lines and jumped to the walk. He was big, around thirty, a heavy beard showing blue-black against swart cheeks and jaw, even though he had shaved recently. His arms were long, his forehead low, the black eyes a little close together. Sam Allee judged he would be a wicked barroom brawler. His hair was tousled when he peeled off his hat in front of the girl.

"You Miss Bollen?" At her nod he went on. "I'm Hank Lofter, Drake's foreman. Sorry to be late. We threw a wheel on the buggy and had to go back for the wagon." He settled the hat on his head again, raking Sam Allee's deceptively slender body with hard, bold eyes. "Who's he?" Lofter had not been on the ranch when Sam had left the country.

The harsh tone made the girl evasive and she said only, "He was on the stage. He helped with my bags."

"Take them, Bert," the foreman told the rider on the ground, his eyes still on Sam. "Thanks. But don't try to move in any closer. Who are you and what are you doing here?"

Bert had ducked under the rail, reaching for the cases, adding to Lofter's antagonism his own. "We don't take to strangers in the Park, Mister," he said.

Sam Allee let his bedroll slide, caught the rider's

shoulder, spun him, and slammed him against the hitch rail, saying sharply, "Don't crowd me."

The group from Drake's ranch froze. The sitting figures before the saloon watched more alertly, the brown paper cigarettes that had dangled from their mouths tipping up at the promise of a fight. A fight would be entertainment, the best they could imagine.

Bert shoved off from the hitch rail, his hand dropping to the butt of the gun in the worn holster.

Hank Lofter's rough voice stopped him short. "Lady present, Bert."

The hand went rigid, then lifted away slowly so there could be no mistaking his intention. Reluctantly the tension went out of him, but his eyes were hot on Allee.

"Nobody puts a hand on me, mister. Clear out."

"Never mind. Never mind." Lofter's tone was a whipcrack. "Get her gear in the wagon. Miss Bollen, we brought an extra horse in case you'd rather ride."

She sounded nervous, unsettled by the near-violence. "No, Mister Lofter, there'll be time to get used to the western horses later." She turned her back on him, thanked Sam Allee, then permitted the foreman to lift her to the wagon seat.

When the two cases and the trunk were loaded, Lofter ordered Bert to drive her to the ranch, leaving a horse for himself. His mouth held in a tight line, Bert climbed beside the girl, turned the team, and went back up the street at a run. Not until he had turned the corner out of sight did Lofter look again at Sam Allee.

"I asked you a question. What are you doing in North Park?"

Sam did not mean to advertise, particularly to his brother's foreman. He said easily, "Looking for a ranch for myself."

"You'll find nothing for sale here."

"I can try."

"I wouldn't. Look somewhere else. Bert isn't

going to forget you roughing him around, and he's a bad man with a grudge."

"Thanks, but I don't like to be crowded."

"Few do. Few want to push the Kid either. The stage south goes out in half an hour."

Lofter dropped off the walk, mounted the horse Bert had ridden in, and with the two remaining riders bringing the black animal, began a dash out of town in a boil of dust.

2

It was more nearly a corridor than a room, so sheltered under the wooden gallery roof that an oil lamp burned in a bracket at the rear. Sam Allee stepped through the door, carried his bedroll the empty length to the high desk under the lamp, and tapped the bell there.

Sound came through the open door connecting the lobby with the barroom—voices, then footsteps that brought a fat man who squeezed between Allee and the stairway newel post to get behind the desk.

Allee said, "A room for a few days. Best you have."

"Ain't no difference except the corners got two windows," the fat man wheezed. A frayed toothpick jiggled in one side of the cupid's-bow mouth. He turned the school notebook ledger and offered a pen, a chicken tail-feather quill cut on an angle and slit at the end. Allee poised it above the page for a second, then wrote in a bold script: Samuel Allee, El Paso, Texas.

The man behind the counter read upside down, his mouth pursing further, leaking a little saliva where the toothpick hung. He raised his eyes again.

"Thought so soon as I saw you, but I couldn't believe it. Drake know you're back?"

Allee's twisted grin mocked himself and the màn. "I doubt it. But as quick as you get back to the bar the news will spread in a hurry. You'll let him know."

The fat man looked hurt, and his voice rose, shrill in protest. "Sam, that ain't fair. I never took sides. Man in my position can't. I got to draw my customers from everybody."

The last word was a pained wail. Achey Collins was the Park's crybaby, which was why he was known by the nickname instead of "Elmer" as his mother had christened him.

Still pained, he added, "It's a risk, you coming in here again. You think Drake is going to be happy you're in the Park?"

Sam Allee laughed at him. "I know damn well he won't be, and, my fat friend, I do not care what Drake Allee feels about where I am."

He took the key and climbed the stairs, leaving Achey Collins wriggling out from behind his desk to hurry to the bar with his news. Room number eight was at the northwest corner of the building, and he must have been given the key out of habit. The door would not quite close, let alone lock. Bullet holes made a scorched pattern in the cheesecloth glued against the ceiling boards; the windowpane was cracked. This was Achey's best room? Sam crossed to the window and heaved at the sash until it gave and rose, shrieking. Three feet below, the roof of the kitchen lean-to sloped. Sam's lips lifted at one side. Achey Collins had located him here with an escape in case Drake decided to come after him.

Their feud went back as far as Sam could remember. It was rooted in his half brother's childhood hatred that had early infected Sam as well. Drake had never forgiven Sam's mother for marrying their father. She had been the hired girl who cared for the ailing first Mrs. Allee. When Drake's mother died, the father had taken Nora Sharkey as his wife. A year later Sam was born. From the first Drake saw the new baby as a threat to his position as sole heir. At every opportunity he sneered to Sam that the marriage was no more than the cheapest way to keep a cook on the ranch.

Sam never learned if there was any truth in the accusation. He knew very little about his mother, and because his father would not talk about her, all he knew he had read in her pitifully few papers. One letter revealed that his father had paid her passage from Ireland. It was not uncommon for some lonely farmer or rancher who needed a servant to send money to bring an Irish girl across the ocean and across the country, bonding her to work out the cost over a period of years. Nora had served the family until Sam was five; then she was killed in a fall from a horse. From then on, the kitchen, the heart of the ranch house, was ruled by Hi Sing, an ageless Chinese who had cooked for the crew, a harsh disciplinarian.

Sam's had not been a happy childhood. There was no appeal from Hi Sing's edicts; Drake had tormented him with endless small cruelties; their father had ignored him as if sight of him were a painful reminded of the lost Nora. Then, when he was seventeen the father was trapped in an avalanche while trying to rescue some winter-bound stock, and Sam and Drake were orphans.

There had come the cold morning when the half brothers in their sheepskin-lined coats had sat in Judge Pell's chilly office, across from the wizened man bundled in a heavy shawl. Pell had settled his rimless glasses on his thin nose, peered over them at Sam, and said in his nasal voice, "What I have to tell you, boy, will come as a shock, but your father had his reasons."

Foreboding froze Sam further as he saw Drake's arrogant smirk, and the lawyer cleared his throat in fussy disapproval before he continued.

"You, Sam, are under age and it would require a guardian to administer a share in the estate. Furthermore, your father was displeased at your friendliness with the hill people, which indicated lack of judgment. Therefore both he and I deemed it wisest that Drake inherit the ranch entire. These are hard times in the Park, and if he is to hold Seven Rivers together at all, he will need a free hand in its management."

The triumph on Drake's handsome face had told Sam his half brother was already aware of the will's stipulation. He thought it probable that Drake had had a hand in the decision.

In a voice flat and toneless to hide his sudden anger he said, "Drake wins it all, and I am squeezed clear out."

The lawyer coughed. "No, no, you are jumping to conclusions. I am confident that when you mature, Drake will make you a full partner."

"Sure he will." The sarcasm was too clear to miss. Drake chuckled.

Pell colored and added quickly, "In the meantime your father did leave you a token."

"What? A worn-out saddle?"

"You are being difficult, Sam. He leaves you five thousand dollars."

Five thousand. Sam's tight mouth dropped slack. He who had never had more than a couple of dollars at one time in his life. He asked suspiciously, "To be withheld until I'm twenty-one? And if I crawl to Drake?"

"Neither." The prissy voice bit out the words now. "It will come to you as soon as the estate is probated. Within thirty to sixty days. Now go along both of you, I have a case to work up."

Sam stood, a bomb exploding in his head. He had been a prisoner on Seven Rivers, an underpaid rider who drew the dirtiest chores. Suddenly he was freed, with five thousand dollars, the world and life before him. To hell with the ranch, with Drake, with North Park and all of Colorado.

On the snow-clogged street he challenged his half brother. "I suppose you didn't know a thing about it."

Drake sneered at him. "What do you think I've been doing for years?"

"Cheating. Lying. Making a big thing out of the time I spend in Kings Canyon, to euchre me out of my share in Seven Rivers."

Drake Allee laughed outright, an unpleasant, victorious bray, and taunted, "You don't deserve a share, an Irish lout whelped because my father got tired of sleeping alone and took a biddy to bed."

Sam hit him without forethought, broke his nose. Bright blood jetted and dyed the snow. Drake swung, blinded; the blow missed and Sam came boring in with unleashed fury. Five years younger and slighter than his brother, the sudden explosion and momentum of the attack gave him advantage. There was no use hammering at the big body armored in the heavy coat. The only vulnerable target was the face, and Sam stabbed at that with quick piston strikes. Dancing in the slick underfooting, slipping now and then but managing not to fall, he cut Drake down methodically, jabbing at him until the bigger man dropped forward like a felled tree and lay unmoving, face down in the churned, pink snow. Sam stood over him gasping. The thin mountain air, the below-zero January temperature did not deliver enough oxygen to his laboring lungs. He felt that his pounding chest would blow apart, that his heart was far too large for his body.

His temptation was to leave Drake where he lay; hopefully he would freeze to death. But something inside Sam deeper than his rage would not let him walk away. With the last of his fading strength he stooped, wrapped his fingers in the coat collar, dragged Drake across the street and into the heat waves of the hotel barroom, where he dropped him on the floor under Achey Collins' astonished eyes. The sudden heat made him giddy. He wanted to hang onto the bar for support, but pride kept him back. If he could have used the excuse of wanting a drink he would have done it, but because he was underage the barman would not have served him, and that would have galled him further.

Without speaking to anyone he turned about and, walking carefully to avoid staggering, went back to the street. The cold there revived him enough so that he could climb the stairs to Judge Pell's office above Finnegan's store. The lawyer looked up in surprise at seeing him again so soon.

Sam told him in a tired monotone, "When that five thousand is ready, send a message up to old Doc Wertz's place in Kings Canyon. I'll be there."

The man's face pinched in disapproval. "I don't believe that's wise, Samuel, but we should expect it of you."

"It's wise all right. I just knocked Drake cold, and he'll want my scalp. I don't want to have to kill him, but I might if I stayed around here. You get me the word. If I don't hear in sixty days, I'll come down looking for you."

He went out then, down to his horse, mounted and let it carry him to the ranch, sagging in the saddle, exhausted by the tempest of anger and the exertion of the fight.

In the Seven Rivers bunkhouse he was throwing gear into his war-bag when Hi Sing opened the door, watched for a second and shouted angrily, "What you think you up to now?"

Sam told him in no uncertain terms. The Chinese ran back to his kitchen and brought a cleaver, brandishing it, yelling that Sam was not going anywhere near that no good hill tribe, blocking the doorway.

Sam had worn a forty-five at his hip since he was twelve when he had begun working with the herd. It was not for fighting. Any mounted man handling cattle needed a gun in case of accident. He drew it now as the Chinese danced and shrieked, then fired twice into the floor short of the blue slippers, and again between the quilted trouser legs as Hi Sing, crouched in the spraddle of an Asian warrior, held the wedged blade as a sword at shoulder level. The piercing chatter of the voice cut off momentarily. Then the Chinese flung about and ran across the yard, yelling in a language Sam supposed he had forgotten after the years in this foreign country.

Sam was surprised at himself for laughing. For all the hostility, he had a warm place in his heart for the bossy cook, the only person since his mother's death who had shown any interest in the boy's welfare. Yet Hi Sing had been a tyrant, and Sam Allee had had enough of tyrants.

Two of the horse herd were his own, bought from the meager wages his father had allowed him. One he was riding today, already saddled. He caught up the other, slung on a packsaddle and the war-bag, and rode out of the yard with everything that was his. He did not look back.

The home buildings of Seven Rivers Ranch lay well off the wagon road north and west of both Walden and Cowdry. Young Sam Allee rode first for something to eat at the Cowdry lunchroom, having not relished another encounter in Hi Sing's kitchen. Afterward he took the main road north again to the branch that led east toward Woods Crossing and on to distant Laramie.

Where Pinkham Creek boiled out of the canyon maze he turned along the watercourse. The tie-cutters had hacked the narrow, twisting track out of the timber in order to haul their logs. A mile of that brought him to the true mouth of Kings Canyon. This was a world apart. Here Doc Wertz had built what he called his homestead, a dozen cabins set at haphazard angles with no defined street.

Once there had been a mine a mile higher in the mountains. When Doc Wertz with his sons and nephews had first come to North Park, they had found no room to establish themselves and had retreated to the mine and tried to live there. After two winters they gave up. The mine road was crossed seven times by the creek, and both years the melting snows churned down, washing out the bridges that had taken so much labor to build.

So the community had moved downhill. That had angered the Park ranchers, convinced them that Wertz and his ragtag relatives were rustling their beef. None of them had been caught at it, but an ultimatum was delivered telling them to move on out of the country. Doc ignored it. The big ranchers sent their crews to burn out the hill people, some fifty riders against Doc and his fifteen men. When the battle smoke cleared, twenty ranch hands lay dead and the rest ran, some to lick their hurt pride at home with their outfits, others to keep going. Doc never admitted to the loss of a single man.

How did they maintain life? They ran a few head of cattle in the upper reaches of the canyon where the steep walls kept them from straying. Doc horrified the Park by running several hundred sheep with them. But those animals were to bring in cash income. The colony's food came from hunting and trapping. Venison was free for the taking, so abundant that when the snows rose so deep the deer could not feed, hundreds of them starved every winter. Also, the swales were filled with shallow beaver dams where thousands of the industrious animals grew thick coats of fur for Doc and his men, to keep them warm and to barter.

Doc Wertz had no use for Drake Allee or his father, but the lonely Sam had been accepted and was free to roam the canyons and hills. It was here he retreated now to await his inheritance.

He rode in, hung his horses at the broken rail in front of the log store where Doc carried a small stock of flour, bacon, beans, tobacco and whiskey. Doc was sampling a new keg when Sam came in, rolling it around his mouth to warm it to full flavor.

Seeing Sam, he choked, spluttered, waved a welcome with the cup and shouted, "Get in this shanty, son, before you freeze solid. How come that uppity brother of yours let you loose on a work day?"

In a grim tone Sam told him about the interview with Judge Pell, of beating down Drake. The little colonist was delighted at the fight, cawing, "I'd have give a lot to see that. Shame you didn't bust the bastard's head. What you aim to do now?"

"Build on the five thousand, Doc. You taught me to play poker, and you're about the only one who can still beat me. I'm going to make a stake to start a ranch on."

Doc's thin face beamed at the compliment. "Did a good job on you, I did. Where you plan to settle?"

"North Park."

The colonist jeered. "Where you think you can find land enough? Every foot is claimed by some greedy bastard that wouldn't give a poor man a chance at a foothold."

Sam's mouth stretched to a tight line. "And only a tenth or less is owned."

"No matter." The little man was bitter. "They got guns to run you out."

"I'll buy guns when I have the stake."

Doc Wertz shrugged. What good to argue with a wild-eyed kid who was not one of the family, not under his control? But he agreed to let the boy wait out the probating at the homestead.

It was the full sixty days before a rider came to report Judge Pell wanted to see Sam Allee. That night he rode to Walden, timing the trip to arrive after midnight when he should not run afoul of some of Drake's crew in town. He threw stones at Pell's window to wake him, then explained by way of apology. Pell grumbled that it was worth getting up in the middle of the night to be rid of Sam for good, dressed and hurried through the bitter night to his office. There he opened the old iron safe and laid on the desk five packets of ten one-hundred-dollar bills each, warning, "Take good care of these. Find a job so you don't spend it all."

"I'll make the most of it, don't worry."

Sam took off his gun-belt, packed the money in the belt around his waist and slapped on the gun again, remembering what else besides poker Doc Wertz had taught him: How to shoot.

Doc had said, "No man is safe playing with tinhorns unless he can protect himself and his winnings."

So Sam had spent hours out behind the cabin store blazing away at chunks of wood set up for him by Doc's eleven-year-old daughter until he satisfied the colonist of his excellence.

Leaving Pell to close the office again, he returned to the community, said his good-byes to the mountain people, threw his gear on his packhorse and continued north to Laramie. There he sold the horses and took the train for what was then the most wicked town in all the west: Denver, across the high mountains to the east.

3

Holladay Street laughed, sang, danced, played, cheated, fought in an orgy around the clock, around the calendar. It was in full throat when Sam Allee stepped into the Criterion and stood at the door to look over the bright, noisy room. His ranging eyes paused on the owner of the saloon, Charlie Harrison, then moved beyond him. Sober, Harrison was a charming Southern gentleman: in his cups his homicidal frenzies earned him a different reputation. He was called deadlier than a rattlesnake. Sam had Bat Masterson's word that not even Wyatt Earp could handle a gun equally with Harrison, and Bat had known them both. As confident of his own ability as Allee was, it was not in his plans to be killed in a drunken barroom brawl and he quietly kept out of the Southerner's way. It was not hard, for his lonely childhood had made him a withdrawn, retiring man who walked largely unnoticed through the throngs.

Sam was here looking for a game and found one at a rear table, slipping into the seat a fat salesman was just vacating. The fat man looked at him with the mournful pity of a bloodhound. Sam took no notice.

He had been in Denver over two years now. Already tall, his slender body had filled out to a solid hundred and ninety pounds. He had lived well, prospered, and fifty-five thousand dollars of winnings lay in the Brown Brothers Bank on Larimer Street. He was getting itchy to be moving, but he had set a goal of one hundred thousand for what he meant to do so he stayed at the tables, never winning too much in one game or one place, keeping his head low so he would not be fingered by the professionals. Yet no week passed that the bank balance did not grow impressively. Six months later a single night brought him to the hundred thousand mark with ten thousand extra for a cushion.

Then he began traveling. He wanted to look at all of the western cattle country, to judge the ranching methods of the different localities. It was another year and a half before he felt he had learned all he could on the ranges and was ready for the next step toward his proposed ranch.

A drought in the Nebraska sand hills east of Denver took him there, where he bought a herd at the depressed price of eight dollars a head. He shipped the steers to Kansas City. They were no good as breeding stock and he took a small loss, but he wanted experience in the sales end of the business. With that under his belt, he lined up a crew, bought a hundred choice animals and started them for North Park as early in the year as the snow would be out of the way. He took on a second crew, the first to trail the animals and later work his range, the other a hardcase crowd to fight. Heading home, he was confident that he had the strength to take back a good portion of the land his brother had cheated him of.

Seven Rivers Ranch was a technical misnomer. There was not a single river on its hundred thousand acres, but its seven creeks made it one of the best-watered ranges in the Park, a lush vale of which Drake Allee owned outright a hundred and sixty acres where the headquarters was built. The rest was open range, but the Park ranchers had gone together and without any legal right allotted each of their number a portion of the government ground.

At the far northwest end of the winding valley near the North Platte stood an empty log house and some buildings falling into disrepair, the roofs sway-backed from snow burdens. The spread had belonged to a James Allen whom Drake had driven off three years before. Sam had run into Allen in Denver, bartending in a saloon, and had bought title to the homestead for one thousand dollars. His first move after the stage had returned him to Walden and he had washed the road dust from his face and hands, was to leave the hotel, walk to the courthouse and have the deed recorded in the county clerk's office.

Ephraim Dole had been clerk for a hundred years it seemed to Sam, a hatchet-faced skeleton whose eyes squinted in alarm when he read the paper; whose voice croaked.

"Does Drake know what you're doing?"

"Not unless he has second sight. Just record it and don't worry."

The man sighed, entered the transfer in his book, and said as he filed the deed, "Your brother won't let you stay there."

"When you tell him, say I'll be at the Allen place waiting for him." Sam paid the fee and left.

The stairs leading up to Judge Pell's office were worn deep as if to prove that the Park's people had found many needs for the lawyer's services. From the courthouse Sam Allee walked the short side-street block, smiling as he climbed the steps, and pushed the door inward without knocking. The rooms beyond were dusty—Sam had never seen them otherwise—and cluttered with papers stacked at irregular angles on top of the big rolltop desk and the long leather-covered table that would look more fitting in a doctor's quarters. Pell peered at the visitor over his spectacles, then took them off, pinching the bridge of his pointed nose as though to dispel an illusion. Sam crossed to the straight chair at the end of the desk, spun it and straddled the seat so he could fold his strong forearms on the back. He rested his chin on them, almost leering at the shriveled, flustered gnome.

"Your bad penny is back, Judge."

Pell tried twice for words, finally managing a chill, "When did you get in?"

"On the afternoon stage, which as usual was an hour late. Nothing much changes in the Park, does it?"

The man choked on a nervous cough and said lamely, "Put on some weight."

Sam kept smiling, not answering the obvious.

Pell gathered himself together to say sourly, "So you spent all that money and came running home to whine."

"I spent my money, part of it. I didn't waste it as you hope. Tomorrow, Judge, I want you to officially notify my brother that I bought the old Allen property and am moving out there."

A concern Sam did not expect puckered the small face, and Pell bent toward him anxiously. "No, Sam, no. Don't try that. Drake has twenty-two riders, and he's using the homestead as a line camp."

Sam Allee rolled his head on his chin from side to side. "Not as of tomorrow morning. My crew is taking over then."

"Your, your, your . . .?" The judge stammered, sounding dismayed.

Sam laughed, straightening on the chair, nodding. "I have more men than Drake has. We'll handle him if he tries to play rough. Judge Pell, I've learned to take care of myself pretty well. Just you give my brother the message."

The judge sat gaping, not answering. After the shock he had just exploded, Sam expected none. He got to his feet and walked out of the dead-silent room. Back on the street he turned into the cross alley, heading for the narrow building where a swinging sign read *Walden News.*

The front window was small and so thick with dust that Ed Kemp kept a lamp lit above the composing stone when he worked there, and since he did all his composing as he set the type, the lamp burned most of the time. Sam Allee saw it as a small, blurred point of light before he opened the rickety door and walked in, calling to the back of the room. Kemp jerked erect, whirling, then whistled a long, low note.

"Well I'll be damned. Old man Jones said he thought he saw you get off the stage but I didn't believe it. Only an idiot would come back to this hick burg after Denver and the kind of feed we had at the Windsor. Remember those oysters? What the hell you doing here?"

Sam remembered the late supper he had bought the editor when he had looked him up after reading in the *Rocky Mountain News* that the Walden man was visiting the city. They had always liked each other. He punched the shoulder, hunched from the years of bowing over the stone.

"First I want to take an ad. I suppose you still publish them?"

"When I can find anybody to pay for them."

"I'll pay. What do you want for a full page?"

The newspaperman laughed at the joke. "What do you want to ballyhoo that big?"

"Give me some paper and a pen if you can find one."

Kemp searched through the litter on one of the two crowded desks, discovered a quill and inkpot, and pawed a clear spot for a sheet of newsprint, then went back to sticking type.

Sam sat down and printed in a bold hand:

ATTENTION ALL RANCHERS AND CATTLEMEN IN NORTH PARK. I, SAMUEL ALLEE, AM HOME. I HAVE

BOUGHT THE OLD ALLEN HOMESTEAD ON MOSS
CREEK, FROM WHICH I INTEND TO RUN SOME
THOUSAND HEAD ON PUBLIC GRAZE. I KNOW OF
THE AGREEMENT AMONG YOU THAT THE
SURROUNDING PUBLIC LAND IS RESERVED TO MY
HALF BROTHER DRAKE ALLEE. NOTICE IS HEREBY
SERVED THAT I DO NOT RECOGNIZE ANY LEGALITY
IN THAT AGREEMENT. I WILL RANGE MY CATTLE
ON AS MUCH AS I NEED.

SAM ALLEE

He carried it to the composing stone and dropped
it before Kemp. The editor's ink-blackened hand
shook as he held it toward the light and read. Then
he dropped it as if it were hot lead.

"You been eating too much raw meat, chump. I'd
as soon blow up the courthouse as run that thing."

Sam said evenly, "But you will run it. You still
publish on Friday?"

"Yes. But not dynamite like this. I want no hand
in getting you killed."

"How much?"

The man looked up in utter disgust, then turned
crafty. If he named a high enough price Sam would
surely back off. He spat the words.

"Five hundred dollars."

Sam Allee knew what this friend was trying.
Without the blink of an eye he fished five one-hundred-dollar bills from his money belt, fanned them,
and dropped them on the stone. Ed Kemp yelped,
gathered the bills into a wad, and crammed them
into Sam's shirt pocket, roaring at him: "All right,
all right. If you want to die this bad I can't keep you
from it, but I don't want your blood money. Why
don't you just draw, shove your gun in your mouth,
and pull the trigger; get it over with."

Sam laughed. "No pleasure in that. Use a heavy
type." He turned away, dropped the wadded bills on

a desk as he passed, and moved out of the little building.

The sun had set, and the early spring evening was chill. He entered the hotel through the bar, paused to buy a bottle, hearing the talk in the saloon fall away, then went through the lobby to the dining room opposite for a supper. The hum of conversation there cut off abruptly and did not commence again until he finished eating and carried the bottle upstairs for two leisurely drinks alone, waiting for darkness.

It was a long ride back through Cowdry, then across Seven Rivers and on to the Allen holding. He wanted to cross the Allee land and pass the head-quarters well after midnight when everyone would be sleeping, which would put him on his new home-stead around noon of the following day.

When the shadows were deep enough to suit him, he took his bedroll and walked to the livery. His trail crew was bringing a *remuda* of horses with the cattle but he needed a mount tonight. The hostler was nervous when he saw Sam Allee, in a hurry to finish the business when Sam said what he wanted. He brought out a chestnut with a white star blaze on its forehead—the horse was named Star, of course—picked the runway lantern off its peg and paraded the animal the length of the long building. Sam trailed behind, studying the good legs, the proud head. At the entrance he caught up, examined the deep chest and said he would take it, then asked about a saddle. As they stood in the barn doorway discussing what was available in the tack room, seven riders came pounding down the street, hoofs drumming dully in the dust.

They had almost passed when one veered aside, hauling his animal up on its haunches, flinging it around, then spurring at the barn, yelling an order to the others. The hostler gasped, dropped the lantern at Sam's feet and wheeled inside. Sam made no move other than to turn slightly to face the street and the charging horseman.

Hank Lofter, Drake Allee's foreman, drove within ten feet of Sam, then danced his horse there while his men spread in a semicircle around Sam, boxing him on three sides.

A rage like a consuming fire burned through Sam Allee, rage at himself, against the smug complacency by which he had allowed himself to be thus trapped. The Seven Rivers men had made one long ride to Walden today to take Drake's fiancé to the ranch. Sam had not thought they would come again so soon. Now he understood that his brother, hearing of his return, was not letting many hours go by before making his attack. If this were tomorrow he would be backed by thirty fighting men. Tonight he was alone. All the odds were that he would not live to see tomorrow.

Bert, the kid he had thrown against the hitch rail at the hotel that afternoon, swung up on Lofter's right, lips pulled back to expose teeth that gleamed hungrily in the lantern glow.

"Captain." The voice was a low threat. "You handled me. Nobody touches Kid Diller. It drives me crazy." He waited for Allee's answer and when he got none, grated, "You got a gun on your hip. Use it. Draw."

Facing the Kid and Lofter, Sam had only a peripheral view of the others. He was confident that he could handle arms as well as any man. He would take Diller and the foreman but there would not be time to hit all in the grinning half-circle. They were not important, only tools; it was Drake behind the fingers almost touching the triggers. It was Drake Allee winning once more, this final time. Sam stood with his hands loose at his sides. He would make it murder, not give them the satisfaction of drawing against an impossible number. There was no other choice, no help to even the chances.

Until another voice intruded. A feminine voice that said, "No, Kid, don't try it. Don't anyone move if he wants to stay alive."

Sam Allee moved nothing except his eyes, casting them as far toward the corral beside the livery as he could strain. He saw a shadowy form behind the rails and the lantern light winked off a long gun barrel shoved between them. She had Lofter and his men quartered. Any one of them would have to turn to make a shot. They sat rigid, none of them risking a move.

She let the silence run until she was satisfied that they understood, then added clearly, "Take off your hats. Hold them over your heads. One at a time, from the far end, use your off hands to drop your gun-belts, but don't move fast or I might get excited and let go with this Greening."

They were sullen but they followed the order, taking care how they used their hands, letting the full belts fall with little sound to the dust of the roadway. When the last weapon lay near the horses' hooves she spoke again.

"Ride out now. Tell Drake Allee what became of your guns. I'll leave them at Cowdry post office. On your way."

Hank Lofter growled at her. "Hell, kid, this is our second ride to town today. We ain't had even a supper, and we're bone-dry."

She was silent a moment, then told him, "Go on to the hotel then, but don't any of you think you can pick up a gun there and try again. The first one comes out the door gets both barrels." The gun barrel tracked them as they dismounted and trailed down the street.

When they had gone inside the saloon Sam Allee faced the corral, saw the dark figure crawl between the poles and step into the circle of light. A small girl with a bridge of freckles and an unruly mop of curling red hair. Sam guessed her about sixteen, developing into womanhood. She watched after the departed riders, then turned to Allee, her grin wide, hitching up the waist of her tan trousers like a cocky boy.

"I've been itching to back that Kid down for a long, long time. He's too fresh with his hands at the school dances."

As his tautness eased Sam's reaction was a laugh at her bantam indignation, then he said soberly, "I'm much obliged. Two more minutes and I'd have been buzzard bait."

Her voice hardened into cold anger with an afterthought. "I wish now I'd shot the lot, the murderers."

"Oh? Who have they murdered?"

"My pop, though we can't prove it."

"Who was your pop?"

Looking startled she sounded disappointed. "You don't remember me?"

Embarrassed, he told her uncertainly, "I'm afraid not. I, well, I've been away five years . . ."

"Milly Wertz. Doc's daughter."

His shock was obvious enough to mollify her. The last time he had seen her she had been a spindle-legged child who had set targets for his practice. The change took his breath.

He said lamely, "You've grown, Milly. How long has Doc been dead?"

"Near two years. I'll tell you later."

They were interrupted by the barn man. Sam had not seen him hurry to the tack room as soon as the Seven Rivers men were gone, but he brought a saddle, heaving it onto the horse Allee had forgotten, sounding short of breath.

"I was you, I'd make myself right scarce around these parts. I'll sell you the animal and the saddle, but I'm not crazy enough to rent. I'd never see either again."

Sam Allee paid the asking price, higher than it

should be. He decided the man was owed something for his fright in the moments when he could have been caught in the firing that had so nearly erupted. While he was paying, the girl ducked back into the corral. By the time he had brought his bedroll and tied it behind the saddle, she was in the street again, mounted, waiting for him, watching the hotel door.

As he stepped up she asked, "Which way you riding?"

"North. And you?"

"Same. Heading home. I had to come down for some medicine for somebody sick at the colony." She turned beside him and they ran the horses out of Walden. "Now about Doc," she volunteered. "We don't know exactly what happened. He and my brother Rob were out hunting. You remember where Kings Canyon opens out? Well, they crossed the Laramie road there and headed west through the hills above Seven Rivers, through the rough country. They cut a deer trail and separated, following it both ways. After a bit Rob heard a single shot and figured Doc had made a kill. He headed toward where it had come from to help pack the carcass, but Doc wasn't where Rob thought he ought to be, so he fired a signal for Doc to shoot again so he could find him. He didn't get an answer and then he knew something was wrong. It took three hours for Rob to locate Doc's body, shot at close range, in the face. By somebody he knew and wasn't afraid of."

"I am sorry. Doc was a good friend to me." Sam's tone was low, thoughtful. "What pointed suspicion toward Drake's riders?"

"Not riders. Rider. Kid Diller. Two weeks before at a dance at Cowdry schoolhouse he tried to get fresh with me and Doc called him, said if it ever happened again he'd horsewhip the Kid. I think Diller was maybe hunting too, ran across Doc and rode over, probably apologizing so he could get close, and when he was right on top of Doc he shot him. Rob found tracks and trailed them until he lost them way over in the Encampment road. Going straight toward Seven Rivers."

Sam Allee looked up at the arch of stars, enormously distant, and the loneliness of his childhood filled him again. Loss of Doc Wertz brought a personal pain. Part of his homecoming had been the anticipation of seeing the wiry little man so filled with vitality, the man who had taken in the stray and taught him so much. They rode half a mile saying nothing, Sam's silence a last tribute.

When he was in control of his voice again he asked softly, "Who runs the store now? Who's head of the colony?"

There was irritation in her answer. "My brother Rob handles the store. Old Uncle Tom claims to lead the people but he's a bully and not as smart as Doc was. The cousins don't take his orders well. They're not together like they used to be."

Again they were quiet. Sam remembered the irascible Tom and tried to picture discord developing in what had been a close, disciplined family community. His loneliness turned bitter. Then some of that lifted. The girl at his side had rescued him, an act of friendliness that had put her life in danger. He smiled across and it lightened his voice.

"I'm a lot luckier than Doc, with you happening to be on hand to save my neck. Coincidences like that don't grow on bushes."

"Not entirely a coincidence, Sam. I'll confess. I was in the barn when you came and started talking to Albert, Otto's new partner, about renting a horse. I kept out of sight because, frankly, I was curious about your coming back. I waited for you to finish dickering, to ask him what you'd said. Then he came running, whispering that Lofter and Diller and them had you cornered and to keep down. I grabbed his shotgun out of the office and ducked through the corral door. Are you going to try to stay in the Park?"

"I am. This is my home. I mean to have my place here."

4

The early morning sparkled, insects sang happily in the deep grass, the creek at the foot of the meadow gurgled, purred to itself in its hurry to join the North Platte a mile across the flat. Joe Hunter ambled naked toward the stream, whistling his pleasure, swinging a towel in one hand.

He knew he was the luckiest man alive. Stationed at the old Allen homestead that Seven Rivers now used as a line camp, his chores were riding fence and keeping an eye out for animals in trouble. It was anything but arduous work. Once in awhile he found a strand of wire down and stapled it back in place. Occasionally he came on a cow tangled in the fence, cut her free, and daubed her cuts with tar against worms. His time was as much his own as he could imagine. Once a month another rider brought fresh grub and relieved him so he could have his day in town. Joe would come back the following morning red-eyed and exhausted, knowing that as soon as the relief rider was gone he could curl in the sun on the lush green, sweet-smelling grass carpet and make up the lost sleep.

At the edge of the water he dropped the towel and stooped for a flat stone at his feet to skip across the surface, purely because he felt good. As he straightened, the musical jingle of harness on the still air made him turn. A long line of horsemen in single file was just rounding the shoulder of the hill that towered behind the line camp. Before he could make out faces Joe thought that for some reason Drake Allee was sending the full Seven Rivers crew to this end of the range. As they came closer he saw they were strangers. Not the hill people anyway. They avoided Seven Rivers unless by ones and twos they slipped in for a beef. He did not know who these were.

Uneasiness came. Joe Hunter swept up the towel and made a long-legged dash for the log house. The leading rider spurred his horse and swerved across to block the way, pulling a rifle from the boot at his knee. Joe skidded on the grass in an abrupt stop. He wished to God he had the guns from the house a hundred feet away. With no defense except what dignity a stark naked man could command, he drew himself up facing the rider, demanding, "Who are you? What do you want here?"

The man on the horse was big, ugly, grinning. "Now ain't you a picture, and trespassing too."

Joe Hunter's mouth fell open. "Trespassing, hell. You been eating loco weed or you lost? This is Seven Rivers' line camp."

The rider wagged his head slowly. "Wrong, you scrawny picked chicken. This is headquarters for Samuel Allee's new ranch. You got ten minutes to pull on your boots, stow your gear, saddle your horse, and clear off."

Joe Hunter's mind tilted off its axis. If this was a joke it was a bad one. The line camp was filled with Seven Rivers property. He started to argue, stopped as the other riders surrounded him and walked their horses at him, forcing him to give way toward the house. He shrugged and turned, crossing to the door.

He did not intend to leave, give them the place free. He was in charge until his foreman or Drake

Allee gave him contrary orders, and he would protect this place as best he could. He did not think of
himself as brave. His gratitude to Drake was deep
for his life here, and his training was to defend the
ranch's interests at all times. That was the code of
the land, the reason why a simple forty-dollar-a-
month man would fight and die rather than let any
harm come to his outfit.

The second he was through the door he slammed
it, diving for the rifle in the deer-hoof cradle above
the fireplace. He had it in his hands, turning,
pumping in a shell when Butch Rathbone shot him
through the closed window.

Hunter fell slowly, still turning, the rifle clattering
on the floor, blood spilling out of the gaping hole in
his bare ribcage.

Rathbone watched the fall and the way the body
lay still, without twitching at all. The shot had been
true and not deflected by the glass. He slipped the
rifle back in its boot, not needing to glance down to
see that it too dropped true. He lifted his leg across
the horse's rump and stepped down. Around him the
others got stiffly out of the saddles. It had been a
long ride and they were sore and weary. They
moved into the big room, crowding it. Rathbone
picked up Hunter's gun, examined it for quality, laid
it across the hoofs, then delegated two men to carry
the body out behind the barn and plant it.

Only one among them protested. "You didn't need
to kill him. You could have winged him."

Rathbone's eyes glittered. "He went for the rifle,
didn't he?"

"Any man worth his salt will fight for his outfit."

"Against thirty guns? There ought to be a limit to
loyalty."

The crew brayed a laugh. They knew Rathbone
and he knew them. There wasn't a rougher crowd in
the Jackson Hole country where Sam Allee had recruited them. They were outlaws, not one in ten

using the name he had started with. They had understood at once what Sam was proposing and had not hesitated to sign on. Their job here was solely to fight off Seven Rivers until Sam had his new brand thoroughly established.

The herd was being driven south by a crew of regular riders Sam had hired in Nebraska at the time he bought the cattle, men who would not be expected to fight.

Sam had slipped across Seven Rivers through the black early morning hours and arrived at the Allen homestead just as the cook who had taken over the line camp kitchen was sweeping the metal bar around the inside of the iron triangle, calling in the men for the noon dinner. Greetings were put off until after they had eaten. They gorged in silence, their appetites huge. When they were filled, Sam and Rathbone sought privacy at the corral, rolled smokes, and sat down against the fence. It was a small holding pen, already filled with the horses Rathbone's men had ridden and the spares they had driven ahead of them.

Sam Allee swallowed a drag of smoke, let it out through his words. "Any interference?"

Rathbone's lip curled. "Man alone here when we rode in. Told us we were trespassing. He's buried behind the barn."

Sam Allee grunted disapproval. A mere line rider who probably had owned nothing more than a change of clothes and a worn saddle.

"Couldn't you have just kicked his tail off the place?"

Watching Rathbone's mouth turn down Sam thought this was the ugliest man he had ever seen, the picture of a born killer, low forehead, greedy, piggish eyes, brutal lips. Even his hands were ugly, with square-tipped, knobby fingers. The wonder was that they could handle a gun expertly enough to have won a dangerous reputation. His voice was a surly growl.

"He pulled a rifle on me. You don't like it, I'll ride on."

Rathbone was secure in the threat. He had Sam by the short hairs, a man bringing in a thousand head of feeders, needing grass to throw them on, and the only way to get grass was to force a brother off a part of what he claimed. He did not wait for an answer.

"When you expect the critters?"

Sam ignored the threat, said evenly, "They were unloading them at Laramie when I came through. It's fifty miles from there to Cowdry and maybe twenty here. Say seventy miles. With luck they'll make about ten a day but it's safer to figure five. A couple of weeks, and there's a lot to be done before they come in."

Rathbone flipped his cigarette stub in an arc. "Such as?"

"Make more room, throw up another bunkhouse and cook shack to separate your people from the working crew. Build more holding corrals and start repairing the outbuildings."

Rathbone snarled his objection. "We didn't sign on to do no building chores."

The showdown had to come, and the sooner the better. This man was vicious, but Sam needed him and his kind if he were to carve his place in this lush Park. He also needed to command control. He laughed, a short, sharp, mocking sound.

"Use your head, Butch. You signed on to establish a ranch. That includes a headquarters big enough to house everybody, feed everybody and keep your fighting crew out of squabbles with the riders. We can't do the job with people at each other's throats, and if we don't do it, if that herd gets here with ten more men and we're not ready, there'll be a mess that will get us all laughed out of

the country." Ridicule, Sam knew, would be intoler-
able to Butch Rathbone. "So your boys had better
pick up some hammers. Take them in to Walden to
buy wagons, lumber, tools, a range big enough to
cook on for thirty men and kitchen equipment,
stores to eat on. Get all you need in one trip and get
back here before Drake knows you're around. Stay
together so you won't be bushwhacked one or two at
a time."

"Teach a dog to suck eggs." Rathbone sneered,
then he studied Allee with a grudging respect. "You
got a head on your shoulders at that. How do we get
to Walden without going across Seven Rivers or
around Robin Hood's barn the way we came in?"

"Follow Allen's lane. That's Seven River's south
boundary, following the creek, and if you spot anybody you can move into the trees there." He rose,
starting to the corral gate to catch up a fresh horse.

Rathbone called, "You going someplace say
where."

Allee turned back. "Kings Canyon to talk to some
mountain people. I want them on our side, not
against us."

He ducked between the rails, located the big animal he had bought in Nebraska, lifted a rope off the
gate post, and tossed a loop. The horse did not fight
it nor fight the saddle. Sam led it out, fastened the
gate, mounted and took Allen's lane. It would cut
the main road just south of Cowdry. It was supper
time when he reached the lunchroom. He stopped
there for coffee and a sandwich.

Behind the counter Mrs. Devers was in a kitten-
ish, teasing mood, normal to her. Sam had known
her most of his life, knew there was no escape and
submitted in good humor. She served him, then bent
over the counter, leaning on her elbows.

"That girl come in with you off the stage, she's a
real looker. One to give a young man like you ideas,
Sam."

He knew Emma Devers' scurrying curiosity would have identified Martha Bollen and her reason for being in North Park, probably the evening before, knew he was being baited, and made no comment. He did not want to talk about the blonde girl with anyone since he craved her so much and was being summarily denied even a chance with her.

Emma Devers made her educated guess and gave him an arch look, cutting deeper. "I hear she's come out to marry your brother?"

Sam Allee put down his rise of temper. News in this territory traveled on the wind, helped along more than somewhat by this magpie in the station where the stages stopped twice a day. He forced disinterest into his tone.

"That's what she told me."

The woman's expression became shrewd. "Drake know you're in the Park again?"

"He knows, all right."

She bent closer, pressing her questions. "You mean to try to stay?"

Allee stood up, backed away, his face empty, swallowed the coffee dregs as he rang a half-dollar on the counter top. "I might and I might not."

Leaving the flat words hanging, he went out to the horse, untied it, lifted himself to the saddle, and continued north on the Laramie road as it paralleled the southwest course of turbulent Pinkham Creek on his right. A few miles further the creek veered away through a lightly timbered delta that dropped gently from the narrow mouth of Kings Canyon proper. Shortly thereafter a wagon trace that connected the mountain community with the road crossed a cattle guard just before the intersection. Iron rails laid on a wooden frame made a barrier cattle would not cross. The horse disliked the footing when Sam Allee turned into the trace, took it with mincing steps that rang metallically as its shoes struck the rails.

At the top of the delta just short of the canyon,

the scattered cabins of most of the Wertz tribe clustered at the edge of the heavier timber of the rising mountainside. Allee rode leisurely, not pushing the animal up the grade, reaching a point where a nose of the hill jutted out to the trace. There a sharp voice called to him to stop. He hauled up the roan, looking toward the sound. Milly Wertz walked out of the bush with a rifle steadied on his middle.

"That's far enough. Turn around."

His mouth dropped open. This was the girl who had saved his life when the Seven Rivers crew had him whipsawed, had talked so friendly less than a day before. In astonishment he asked, "Why? What's the matter here?"

She said tensely, "You're not wanted in here now, Sam. Ride out."

"But I . . ."

She moved the gun only enough to call attention to it. He stared at her, not comprehending, saw color come hot into her face, and tried again to speak, but she shook her red hair and nodded down the canyon.

"Don't argue with me, Sam Allee. Go on. Now."

5

There was nothing for it but to turn the horse down the way they had come and appear to give up his errand. He did not know what had caused the abrupt about-face in Milly Wertz's attitude toward him, wondered if she were acting on old Tom's orders. If that were so, Sam Allee would have more problems cut out for him than he had counted on. The hill people surely would not join his brother against him, but while he and Drake were fighting each other the tribe might take it into its collective head to step up the rustling he had always assumed they practiced on the closer ranches.

He crossed the cattle guard again, paused on the road to look back and to raise an arm to the redhead still standing where he had left her. She lifted a hand tentatively in answer, and he welcomed that as a signal that she was not personally angry at him. But he needed to find out more clearly just where he stood with the others. He headed back toward Cowdry, but when he had gone far enough for the trees on the lower mountain that bracketed the delta to hide him and Pinkham Creek ran wider, slower than it did above, he forded it and turned back uphill.

From his early days of roaming this country he remembered that there was another ford opposite the cluster of cabins and the store, a place where a submerged rock dike impeded the churning water so that an area of gravel had built up wide enough for horses to cross. The trouble with using that was that it was in full view of the store yard and he would more than likely be spotted. But beyond that there were other ways over by foot. The trail that went up the much-narrowed canyon to the abandoned mine wove back and forth. Great logs lay felled across the water, their upper sides adzed to make footbridges. Sam Allee rode to the first of these.

He tied his horse out of sight within the trees and from their shelter, close to the stream, looked back down on the trampled, sunbaked yard in front of the store. There was no one in sight, no horse at the hitch rail. He left his rifle with the saddle and in his high-heeled boots stepped out to tackle the log that was wet and slippery with spray. Balancing, pigeon-toed, keeping his eyes on the unmoving ground of the far side, not looking down at the rush and swirl of white water beneath him, feeling for footing, he picked his way across.

When he came down to the yard no one had yet appeared. He ran lightly across it to the store, went up the steps to the high gallery, and walked boldly through the open door. No one was inside either he saw, his quick glance sweeping the cluttered room. There was no order in the shabby building. Goods lay in indiscriminate piles on low counters, on sagging shelves against the walls, in heaps on the splintered floor, making it hard to find walking room. Allee listened but heard no signs of life. Since there was no rear door, he went out by the way he had entered and circled the store cautiously, not wanting to surprise anyone. He had been warned not to come here and the Wertz crowd's reactions were unpredictable. At the back corner he stopped and looked around it toward the big barn where the community's horses were kept stabled.

In the yard a man squatted over a dead steer, cutting out a forequarter. He was facing away from Allee and unaware of his arrival. Spread on the ground beside the man lay the brown hide of the animal, the brand plain to read. The Allee Seven Rivers mark, seven wavy parallel lines burned deep in the skin.

Some sixth sense appeared to warn the butcher that he was no longer alone. His head turned slowly, reluctantly, as if he were afraid of what he would see. Then he froze, staring into Sam Allee's quiet face. Sam recognized Milly's brother Rob Wertz. Six feet away. A moment passed, then Rob swiveled and launched himself up and forward in a spring of his powerful legs, the bloody, thick-bladed butchering knife extended forward and murder in the muddy eyes.

Sam's first instinctive reaction was to drop his hand to the butt of his short gun, but he stopped before he drew. In the brief second of time he had in which to make his choice, it flashed on him that if he shot the young man he would kill any hope of help or neutrality from the kinsmen. Beyond that, it would kindle a blood feud that would burn until he himself was killed or the mountain tribe was wiped out, which Sam Allee wanted no part of. Yet Wertz had to be stopped fast, before the lunge brought him bulling into Sam and the red, dripping knife was plunged into his belly.

A big cottonwood grew near the building corner. Sam jumped for that, flinging himself behind it. At least Rob wore no gun, though the butchering blade was wicked enough. Wertz brought himself up short, panting, eyes blazing; then, in a crouch, his legs wide apart, he stalked forward, moving around the tree bole as Allee circled it away from him.

"Allee, I'll carve your guts out when I catch you."

"Quit it, Rob. Listen. I don't give a damn how many Seven Rivers beeves you take. For all I care you can have the herd. Put that knife down and hear what I came to say."

Rob Wertz might have been deaf. Sam's words did not penetrate through the haze of shock the sight of Sam had given him. He came on, weaving, step after step around the thick trunk.

Sam's voice slammed at him again. "Rob, stop it. I could have shot you. I still could, but I won't. I don't want you dead. I want to talk."

Still Rob Wertz appeared not to hear a word. He showed no reaction. Like some unstoppable, unthinking monster he moved toward Sam, full around the tree two times. On the second circle Sam drew his gun and threw it as far as he could, making sure Rob saw what he did. If Wertz broke off to run after it, Sam could jump him from behind, club him behind his ear, and knock him out. But Wertz did not take the bait; so intent was he that his eyes did not even flick to the arc of the gun through the air. And now Sam was empty-handed. It came down to which of them could hold out longer at this grim game, and

Wertz looked as if his strength were a match for Sam's.

Then Allee saw the thin-bladed skinning knife stuck in the ground behind the pegged-out hide. He feinted around the tree toward Wertz, and when Rob set his feet for another lunge, Sam swung away. In three running steps he had the haft in his hand, had pulled the knife free, and had swung to face Wertz, the blade held low and level.

He shouted, "Rob. Hear me."

Wertz stopped, but for a second only. Then he was advancing with his crouching roll, slow, cautious, his attention caught at last by the skinning knife. Allee moved then in a rush, charging, seeing the butcher knife pushed forward, pointing for Allee's middle. At the last instant Sam swerved and clamped his empty left hand around Rob Wertz's thick wrist behind the butcher knife. He tried to twist it, to wring the hand until the fingers dropped the blade. Wertz was too strong, too fast. In a flashing move he switched the butcher knife to his left hand, wrenched his right loose, and caught Allee's knife wrist in a vice grip, in his turn twisting but with no more success than Allee had had. Allee's free fingers fastened on the other's left arm.

They stood toe to toe, all four hands straining to break the grips. Then Allee raised his left foot, hooked it behind Wertz's leg, and threw his weight forward against the man, knocking him over backward. They fell heavily, together, Allee partially on top but neither grip was broken. They lay thrashing, rolling, hanging on. Both were powerful men, both were skilled at rough-and-tumble fighting, and the battle could have raged on until one must weaken. Then it would end in a death or a crippling wound.

A rifle shot close at hand stopped it. A furious voice made both look toward it. In the sudden stillness Milly Wertz commanded, "Quit this, both of you. Drop those knives."

Neither obeyed, each waiting for the other. She shot again, the bullet kicking dust in their faces.

She said savagely, "If I have to fire once more, it will be into you both."

Allee nodded at Rob, broke the deadlock, let the skinning knife fall, then felt the other's fingers relax. They untangled themselves slowly, both tired and winded, got to their feet watchfully, backed away from the knives on the ground. The girl showed them both contempt.

"You two bullheaded ... children. Sam, I knew Rob had that steer here, that's why I tried to keep you away. I knew there'd be a fight, and one of you could be killed. Rob couldn't know you hadn't made peace with Drake. Now shake hands."

They did but warily and while the handclasp held, five others of the clan ran into the yard, attracted by the rifle fire, armed and ready for a fight. They stopped at a short distance, puzzled, then looked to Milly for an explanation. While she made it Rob picked up the butcher knife, and as if he had lost interest in all of them, went back to cutting out the forequarter.

"You idiot," the girl called after him. "Get rid of that hide before somebody else rides in and sees that brand."

Her brother paid no attention. One of the clansmen took the skinning knife to the pegged hide, slashed the brand out and unconcernedly tucked it in his belt, then went on to the carcass. Rob had the leg severed; he rose and handed the knife to the man, waving in the rest of them. The remainder of the beef was dismembered and shortly the clansmen were gone, each with a share of the meat, untroubled that it was stolen. Rob returned from the timber where he had hung the quarter to cure out of the reach of hunting animals, and went to wash his bloody hands at the horse-trough in the front yard.

Sam Allee too had blood on him from his contact with Wertz and followed to clean himself.

"I came up to tell you, Rob, that I'm home for good. I've bought Jim Allen's spread on Moss Creek that Drake ran him off of and grabbed for Seven Rivers. I'm taking over."

Milly Wertz had trailed Sam Allee and her brother to the trough to be sure they didn't start at each other again. Rob turned his head toward her, surprise wiping his remaining brooding anger from his pulled down mouth, telling in his question to Allee.

"You think Drake would let you get away with that?"

Sam shook water off his hands, wiped them on the torn rag nailed against the trough side, saying flatly, "I'm not asking him. I've got a prize herd coming down in the next few days with a crew to work it. I have another crew already on the place who can handle whatever Drake sends to throw me off."

Something like pleasure glowed in Rob's face, a wolfish hunger at the thought of Drake Allee being challenged by his own half brother; then he turned suspicious.

"And I suppose you want us to help you? Not a chance, Sam. We're not taking on anybody else's war, and you're not one of us even if Pa acted like it."

"I'm not asking that. All I want is an assurance that the Wertz family won't prey on my cattle while I'm tied up with Drake. Your people were always friendly to me, and I don't begrudge you an occasional steer, but if my hardcases catch anybody at it they're apt to hang some of you without my knowing until too late. I don't want bad blood between us."

Rob Wertz's mouth twisted into a sardonic smile, and he chuckled. "Far as I'm concerned we can make out with what we've been finding, Drake's strays. I'll go along, but I don't have the say for the whole family, and if your animals are so much better than his some of the boys might think different."

"Who does have the say now?" He asked the question he had asked Milly, to see if Rob's answer would match hers.

"Pa's brother Tom. Most of the cousins look to him, figure I'm too young to take Pa's place."

Sam Allee heard a warning behind the words and grimaced. He remembered Tom Wertz all too well. The old man had never liked him, never approved of Doc's interest in him, and had never hesitated to make his feelings known to anyone in the hills. But if he hoped to prevent the tribe from provoking retaliation for rustled animals, he would have to put his arguments to the leader, to do his best to convince him of the danger ahead.

"Does Tom still live up at the old mine?"

"Sure."

"Will you and Milly go see him with me? Help me get across to him what can happen?"

The brother hesitated, foreseeing his uncle's stubbornness and not liking the prospect of crossing him, but Milly said at once, "Of course we will. Right away."

"As soon as I find the gun I tossed in the backyard."

It took Sam awhile to locate it, skidded into the brush at the edge of the trees, the barrel choked with loose dirt. He shook it out, broke it, blew it clean, and went back to the Wertz pair. Rob was protesting to his sister, refusing to make the visit, but she put her chin up and started for the trail as Sam came back. Sam said nothing, following the redhead, and before they were out of the yard Rob jogged after them, muttering objections.

They walked. The trail twisted with the curves of the canyon and as the walls narrowed, the bridges of single logs took them back and forth over the tumbling stream. Spring floods had always washed away any crossings that had been built. They washed out these logs too, but one log was simpler to replace than the several needed to take a horse over, so the upper residents contented themselves with hiking. It was only a little more than a mile to the cluster of buildings, but the grade was steep all the way. All three were panting by the time they saw the mine entrance and the overgrown dump. The headframe and the old tunnel entrance were high on the near bank of the stream; on the far side squatted the remains of the bunkhouse that had sheltered a hundred men, the dining hall, the kitchen, and three individual cabins.

Tom Wertz had appropriated the middle one of the three and added another room at the rear, using timbers taken from the decaying bunkhouse. All the buildings were half hidden in a growth of young pole pine and aspen. It was a pretty site, the icy mountain stream filled with firm-fleshed trout, a beaver dam below, the timber full of game—an ideal spot for a man with relatives to supply him to grow old in.

As the visitors crossed the last log, they saw Tom in a broken and mended chair on his porch, a long-haired sheep dog that had been his constant companion as long as Sam could remember curled against his feet. It must be twenty years old. In its youth it had been a fire-eating protector ready to sink its fangs into anyone it thought was endangering its master. Now it was so crippled with rheumatism that it had to struggle to get up and down, so nearly blind that when it rose painfully at the sound of the visitors, its nose bumped hard against a chair leg, almost overturning the rickety seat.

Tom cursed it in a high, cracked voice but made no move to stand, sitting as though on a throne, gnarled hands crossed on the ball of a black-root cane, chin and thinning whiskers resting on his hands. The heavy-lidded eyes were malignant on Sam Allee.

"Ha." The word was a curse as he used it. "You back to pester us, huh?"

Sam stopped at the edge of the porch, not venturing up the step without invitation, surprised to be recognized through the filming eyes, aware that Rob and Milly had hung back.

"How are you, Tom?" Sam tried to sound interested.

Tom grunted in disgust. "How in hell do you think I am? I'm old. Ready to die and the good Lord don't seem to want me." He coughed for punctuation.

Sam lied. "I don't believe it. From the looks of you, you'll live to be a hundred."

"Smart aleck, aren't you? What the hell you doing here?"

Sam Allee told his story, emphasized that he wanted none of the mountain people injured by the hardcase crew he needed to take his ranch away from Drake, asked Tom to see that his relatives stayed clear of the Allen land until he was in firm control. The old man heard him through, not interrupting but rearing against the chair-back like an angry monarch. When Sam finished Tom roared at him.

"You damn fool, bringing scum like that in the Park when you can't handle them. Trying to tell me where we can't go. No sir, as long as I'm alive no Wertz will knuckle under to any Allee. You just clear out of these hills while you're whole and don't come back. You try it and on my word I'll have you shot."

Disappointment, frustration at this despotic willfulness that could wreck his intended peace with these neighbors brought Sam's temper flaring, lashing back.

"You don't own this canyon, these mountains, Wertz. You've squatted here, yes, and maybe you can claim a quarter section, but the rest is government land, land for everybody's use."

The old man bent forward, raised his stick, and whacked it hard on the porch rail as though it were Sam Allee's head. "I'll show you who owns what, you impudent pup." He lifted his voice, shouting. "Hans. Pete."

Two sons had apparently been watching, listening inside the cabin. Both shoved through the door with rifles already leveled on Sam Allee.

"Take him in the mine and leave him there dead."

Sam did not believe he was serious, but the wicked grins on the brothers showed how wrong he was. He was caught flat. Before his hand could drop to his holstered gun there would be at least two bullets in his chest. The men were like vicious twins, with gaunt, long frames and little eyes too close together to indicate any independent thought in their brains. Their ages were two years apart but their intelligences were equally low, no more than animal cunning.

Pete crossed the porch keeping out of the line of fire for Hans, his rifle held loosely in one hand. He came down the step to Sam's side, hooked Allee's gun out of the holster, and shoved it behind the waistband of his own worn pants.

"Turn around now. Over the bridge. Up to the tunnel."

Sam Allee stood still. It seemed incredible that they really meant to kill him in cold blood, but from stories he remembered these mountain men were capable of any brutality. If he were going to die he would do so here, not obligingly climb a hillside to be gunned down and left for animals in the clammy hole in the mountain.

Pete shoved him hard, turned his foot on a stone, and in catching his balance flung his rifle out at arm's length. Another voice cut across the yard, sharp and hard: Milly Wertz.

"Pete, let go of that rifle."

The cousin turned, staring stupidly at the girl aiming her own weapon at him. He giggled. "Keep out of men's business, Sis."

"No. I give you half a minute. You too, Hans. I've got you quartered, and I'm faster than you. You know it."

Suddenly both guns were dropped. Sam Allee understood that these brothers had no doubt their cousin would shoot them. The girl did not give them time to think further.

"Hans, come off the porch. You and Pete move over in front of Tom." When they had obeyed that order Milly told Allee, "Sam, get your gun from Pete. Be careful where you stand. Then pick up theirs."

Allee gathered the weapons, holstered his, broke the rifles, dropped the cartridges in his pocket, tucked the guns in the crook of his left arm.

"Now, Pete," Milly said, "you take the lead down to the store. Hans, you stay here and don't get the idea of fetching another gun. If you do I'll shoot Pete in the back. That is a promise."

After that no one spoke. For once old Tom was without words. That his niece would act against him was unthinkable at first—then Allee surprised an expression on the withered face, a glitter of admiration and pride in the girl's generalship, as though she were proving herself a worthy member of the clan.

Pete glared but he moved out across the yard and the log bridge with Milly just behind him, her rifle still leveled. Rob Wertz nodded Sam next in line, took the rifles from him, and balanced himself with them over the narrow, not quite solid log.

They walked in silence, each nursing his own bitter thoughts. Sam's were on his failure to enlist the friendly cooperation of the mountain people. Equally bad, fuel was now added to the feud that had separated them from his family since before he could remember. They were a proud tribe and that these brothers had been backed down by a girl in front of Allee was gall and wormwood. That the girl was a family member could only aggravate the embarrassment.

They snaked back and forth across the stream, one after the other crossing the logs, and reached the store yard. There the redhead jabbed the rifle in her cousin's spine ungently as a reminder.

"The parade ends here, Pete. Go on home."

The man faced around on Sam Allee, his face murderous, his voice tight in his throat. "If I ever catch you in these parts again I'll skin you and make me a tobacco pouch out of your ass."

The girl jabbed at him again. "Get lost. Now."

He growled at her, "Give me Hans' and my guns."

"You can come here for them tomorrow."

Pete gave up and left, climbing up the rocky trail until he was out of sight. Rob turned and without a word went into the store carrying the rifles. Sam found a crooked smile for Milly.

"Thank you again. It does seem you are determined to bail me out when I get myself in trouble."

She did not smile back. "Where's your horse? Across the creek?" At his nod she told him, "I'll see you that far. Then you're on your own." Her tone came cold. "Don't expect help next time. When you leave here don't come again. You'll die if you do."

They crossed the log. Sam mounted, paused to wave to her, had no answering gesture and turned down the hillside with the sick feeling of being an outcast from the haunts that had given him his only childhood happiness.

6

When Martha Bollen first arrived at Seven Rivers, she was awed at its vastness as Hank Lofter swung a big arm full circle to indicate what the ranch encompassed. The sweeping green, deep meadows delighted her. Approaching the headquarters she was impressed by the number of buildings, barns, large bunkhouse, kitchen and dining hall, blacksmith shop, sheds that made a compact community. Lamps glowing from the dozen rooms of the big house promised a luxury she had never known. And permanent security with a strong, dependable man. It was all so different from the cramped streets and buildings of St. Louis. She would need time to adjust to the openness, but she knew she could be happy here.

Then came fright.

Drake Allee met the wagon in the yard and pulled her off the seat into his arms. But when Lofter blurted his news that Sam was in Walden and had ridden the stage with the girl, Drake forgot her, thrust her away, and gave vent to a rage such as she had never witnessed. He did not notice her again until he had gone with his crew to the corral, watched fresh horses saddled, seen the men ride out again in a rush, on what errand she did not hear. Afterward as he showed her through the house to the bedroom-sitting room suite prepared for her, he was remote and preoccupied. He remained so through their supper, and in a pique she made the excuse of being exhausted by the trip and retired to her rooms to think about this man she was to marry.

At dawn the crew riding in waked her. She dressed, went down the stairs but saw no one, and continued out to the porch. She found a chair near an open window and sat to look across the misted meadows and the hundreds of cows in the near distance. But voices came through the window, Hank Lofter mumbling in a chagrined tone muffled words she could not make out, then Drake's voice in cutting scorn, clear enough.

"You didn't get him. Six big, brave men and you let a scrawny girl brat get the drop on all of you at once? You boneheaded incompetent."

Lofter shouted then. "I ain't so boneheaded I didn't pick up some news in the saloon. The word is your brother bought the old Allen spread and already has a crew moved onto it. Wouldn't you think Hunter would have come in to tell us?"

Martha Bollen counted the minutes of silence. No sound at all came until the slap of a palm on the desk, then Drake, ominously quiet with his words: "That tears it. You take the boys here and round up another bunch from the range. Go over there. Throw Sam and whoever is with him off. If they give you an argument, kill them. I'll handle the sheriff."

Martha Bollen's breath sucked so loudly she feared Drake would hear and discover her listening, but Lofter was speaking again.

"Boss, these boys and I ain't been to sleep since night before last. How long you expect us to keep going at a stretch?"

The reluctant answer came. "All right. If you went now you'd probably not have the wits to do the job. Turn in until noon. But I want this finished before night."

She heard boots tramp out of the room and down the hall toward the rear door. That would be Lofter leaving. Drake would still be there, no more than five feet away. When she had first met Drake she had been impressed by his self-certainty and his strong, square good looks, by his description of the Seven Rivers ranch. Now she was appalled by what she had heard. Would the man she had planned to marry actually have his own brother murdered? It could not be. The word "kill" as he had used it must have some different, lesser meaning in this country, or simply be an exaggeration called forth by his anger at Sam. But she must be certain.

She got up, went into the house and through the door of the room where he was. It was fitted as an office, and Drake sat at the desk stiffly, staring through the window. He turned as he heard her, his face frozen and hard, but when he saw her it broke into the easy smile she knew.

"Did you have a good rest, darling?" he asked.

She ignored that, said directly, "I have to talk with you, Drake."

His smile broadened, and he swung his swivel chair to face her. "There is nothing in the world I would rather do than talk to you. What is it?"

Standing as tall as she could she told him through stiff lips, "I was on the porch, just outside. I couldn't help but overhear what you told Hank Lofter to do. You didn't mean it, did you?"

His smile faded, froze as a grimace, and one shoulder lifted. He did not give a direct answer, said instead, "You'll find some things here that you needn't bother your pretty head about. This is one." It was said evenly enough, but the flat finality of his tone walled her out.

She drew a deep breath, saying as quietly as she could manage, "I realize that I was raised in a very different environment than this and things are alien to me here, but isn't there such a thing as decency even in this wild territory? The Allen ranch was not

yours and you did not buy it. You took it, ran the
man away, just appropriated it. Is that true?"

His eyes narrowed and his voice was sharp. "Who
told you that?"

"Your brother."

"Would you prefer to believe his jealous raving to
what I say?"

"I want the truth. If I must, I can go to the
county courthouse to learn it."

Drake Allee flushed, darkening under his heavy
tan. "I won't have my word questioned by anyone.
Certainly not by my wife. Martha, do not pry into
what is not your affair."

She knew then. His order to Lofter was literal.
Fear became a massive thing within her and an urgency seized her. She must find a way to prevent the
killing. But how? She turned about and went back to
the porch to think. There was only the morning to
act in.

From the first she had had doubts about the marriage. Drake Allee's background was so different
from hers. She had wondered if she would be able to
fit into the raw frontier country, to live on a ranch
miles from town, be for weeks or months without
the companionship of other women. Now there was
this new Drake shutting her out. Her word would
carry no weight with him. Pleading for Sam's life
would not save it. And if she married Drake, there
would be other such times.

But if she refused him, what then? She had almost no money, which had been the principal reason
she had decided on the marriage to begin with. Yet
how could she marry him now?

She heard a sound in the hall and saw him leave
the house by the side door, watched as he crossed to
the corral, caught and saddled a horse, and rode out
without once glancing in her direction. Decision and
opportunity came one on the heels of the other. She
left the porch and rapidly crossed the yard toward

the only sound. A rider was shoeing a horse in the blacksmith shop. All the others at the headquarters were asleep.

She stood in the shop entrance seeing the chain of red-hot sparks spray from the shoe as he hammered it into shape on the anvil, smelling the burning hoof when he put the hot iron against it and nailed it tight. Then, as he finished, she went toward him.

The rider, she remembered his name as Link, saw her movement, looked up and touched his hat. "You want something, Miss Bollen?"

"I want to go to Walden. It's very important. Didn't Drake tell you?" At his head-shake she bit her lip in apparent frustration. "He must have forgotten. He told me you would drive me in."

"Well, sure." He grinned, flattered and pleased to be trusted with the lady. "The buggy's not fixed yet but I'll get the buckboard ready right away."

"Thank you. I'll get my baggage packed. It won't take longer than harnessing." She left and hurried to the house.

Link watched after her with his mouth sagging. Had the lovers had a fight already? How could anyone fight with a girl who looked like this one? If she were his fiancée—but in his most abandoned dreams Link could not imagine Martha Bollen having the slightest interest in a forty-a-month rider.

Twenty minutes later they were on the road. Martha had been tense, frightened that Drake might return before she left. There would surely be a quarrel and she sensed that if it were his pleasure he would hold her on the ranch by force. But they saw nothing of him and reached Walden without being stopped.

At the hotel Achey Collins was startled to see her come in. He knew who she was, had seen her arrival, seen Hank Lofter take her off to the ranch. She asked for a room.

Collins, guessing she had come to town to shop,

turned the old account book, asking as she signed it, "Shall I hold a room for Drake? Is he coming in?"

"Not that I know of. I didn't tell him I was coming."

Link brought in her trunk and bag and waited to hear where to take them. Achey did not like the looks of that, as though she were leaving. He had no desire to run afoul of Drake Allee's temper, and Drake had a bad notion that if a man wasn't with him he was against him. And there was the Seven Rivers crew. He had seen them at work often enough to know that if Drake gave the word they would pull the hotel down around him.

He said cautiously, "Ma'am, I hate to be disobliging, but I can't afford trouble with Drake Allee. Nobody dares to cross that crowd."

She tilted her chin up at him, smiling. "I won't cause you trouble. I'll tell him I made you take me in so I wouldn't have to sleep in the street. You don't think he'd want me to do that, do you?"

Achey Collins felt the trap snap shut on him. Either way he jumped could be bad, but no, he could not turn her out with no stage due until morning, if that was what she had in mind. He pursed his lips in a sort of prayer, handed her a key to an upper floor room, and hurried back to his bar with news that this time he would keep to himself.

Martha Bollen led Link up the bare, scarred stairs to the dismal room, closed the door after he had left, and stood rigidly at the window. Her first thoughts were for herself. She had run on a compelling impulse, and now what was she to do? There was Sam Allee and his easy-to-read interest in her. She could make him marry her, but wouldn't that be jumping from the frying pan into the fire, with Seven Rivers probably at this moment on its way to murder him. She did not think of love, a luxury she could not afford, and this raw, violent land frightened her anyway. The thing to do was to borrow money, return

East, and try to snare a wealthy man there. Borrow from Sam? Jolted by the thought of him, she remembered she must do something to warn him about Drake's order to Lofter, if it were not already too late. She did not know how far it was from Seven Rivers to the Allen place. Sam might be dead by now. But, surely, knowing that his brother would fight him would keep Sam alert, expecting some action.

With that to hope for she hurried out of the room, out of the hotel, grateful that the lobby was empty. She hastened along the hot street toward the livery. She would have gone after Sam herself, but she did not know where his ranch lay. Turning in under the swinging sign that read Otto Schultz Livery she was relieved to find two people in the barn, one obviously the old German owner, the other a boy of perhaps fourteen. The boy was sweeping the runway, but he stopped work to gape, his green eyes wide.

Out of breath, Martha Bollen gasped to him, "I must get a message to Sam Allee at the old Allen ranch. Do you know where it is?" At the bob of his head she added, "Could you take a note out there?"

"Sure can, Miss." He held out his hand.

"I'll have to write it. Is there paper and a pen around?"

"Yeah. In the office." He pointed at the door beside the chair where Otto Schultz dozed.

The man did not lift his head as she passed him on her way into the little cluttered room filled with harness, old saddles, blankets, coils of rope. She pushed a saddle off the chair at the littered desk, sat down, reached for a piece of smudged paper and the eagle-feather quill, dipped that in a pot of congealing ink and wrote:

> *Sam: If they have not already got there, Drake*
> *started his crew at noon to attack you. I heard*
> *him tell Lofter to run you off or kill you. I can't*

marry a man like that and have left. I'm at the
hotel in Walden.

She signed her name and blew the paper dry as
she went back to the runway where the boy was sad-
dling a dun-colored pony. She folded the note and
put it with a silver dollar into his hand. His green
eyes glowed at sight of the money, but he shook his
head, blushing.

"No, ma'am, I don't want no pay to do a little favor for a pretty lady like you."

She had never felt less like smiling but she forced
a curve to her lips. "Take it please, and hurry as fast
as you can. To save Sam's life."

The words rattled the boy and without more argument he shoved both note and coin in his overall
pocket, swung up on the pony, and spurred out of
the barn as though it were afire.

Martha Bollen started back to the hotel with the
sensation that she was holding her breath, that she
could not breathe freely again until she knew
whether the message was delivered in time. Passing
the general store she read a sign in the window—Ice
Cream. She did not really want the sweet but eating
a dish of ice cream would be something to do to
overcome some of her tense restlessness, to turn her
mind from its fears, something to kill the dragging
time.

Inside, the store smelled of fresh-ground coffee,
coils of new hemp rope, a spicy mixture of other
odors. A little man with a black beard covering most
of his face came from the rear expectantly.

Martha Bollen said, "That ice cream sign, do you
really have it?"

"Best there is, ma'am. I made it this morning,
vanilla and chocolate."

She sat down at the single tiny worked-iron table,
saying, "I'd like a serving then, a scoop of each."

7

After the noon meal Hank Lofter took his grumbling, not yet wholly rested crew to circle out over the sprawling Seven Rivers acres and pick up other riders working parts of the herd. He had twelve men behind him when he turned across the range toward the Allen line camp. The afternoon was hot; half the crew was in ill sorts after the long, hard previous day and night; and he did not push them. There was no need to hurry. The quarry would be there like sitting ducks for him whenever he got there. He expected no trouble from them nor that there would be too many for him to handle with the people at his back.

The Seven Rivers outfit was the hardest riding, hardest fighting crew in the entire Park. Drake Allee kept on only tough people, for the small ranchers along the Medicine Bows and around Encampment, to say nothing of the mountain trash, continually preyed on Seven Rivers beef. Only a strong force could generate fear enough to keep them at bay.

Riding at Lofter's side was Kid Diller, Lofter's prize hand and biggest problem. Diller was ruthless, cold-blooded, a natural killer. His temper was vicious although mostly he controlled it. But when something enraged him, then it would blaze forth in sudden violence, or if that were thwarted, it would writhe in serpent coils just below the surface until it found its outlet and erupted. Looking at the tight, thin face, the twitching at the corners of the eyes,

Lofter could almost see the coiling in the narrow chest now. Sam Allee had pushed Kid Diller on a crowded street. Diller had not forgiven that. He was looking forward hungrily to the chance, the excuse, to gun down the younger Allee. Lofter believed the Kid would make that chance today.

His mind pictured the Allen spread, the cabin standing a hundred yards from Moss Creek in as pretty a meadow as could be found anywhere. Lofter had often had the thought that there a man could make an ideal place for himself if he were left in peace, but he always put the idea down as quickly as it came. As long as Drake Allee could keep it so, no one would be permitted to settle there.

Riding toward the place, he knew a sudden mild discontent. The rich got richer and the poor got poorer seemed to be a rule of life. Not that he would be disloyal to the ranch. He had worked for Drake four years now, and Drake had been generous. When he had been made foreman he had been allowed to run two hundred head with the Allee herd, and his stock was multiplying year by year. If only he could shove them onto the Allen land and call it his own ... He shook the dream away before it could poison him.

From the direction of their approach the buildings could be seen a long way off. A curl of smoke rose lazily from the squat chimney so someone was there. No one with half sense went off and left even a stove fire burning unattended in a log cabin. As they rode closer Lofter made out two men moving around the yard near the building, not hurrying, so his crew had not yet been discovered. He took them on at the same easy pace.

Most of Sam Allee's fighting crew were not at the headquarters. Butch Rathbone had the bulk of them in the timber that grew thickly above the valley, cutting logs for the new buildings Sam had ordered. He had not sent anyone to Walden. The cook was in the original lean-to kitchen. David Hunt and Wallie Martin were shoeing horses in front of the blacksmith shop that itself needed major repairs. Joe Gross was at the corral mending a stirrup-strap that had pulled loose. He was the first to see the line of Seven Rivers riders, now almost within rifle range, and he sent a warning shout to Hunt and Martin.

"Look alive. Company."

They had been hired as fighters, and they welcomed the row ahead. All three ran for the cabin, where the cook joined them. Built of thick logs that a bullet could not penetrate, it offered good protection. Each of the four chose a window to fire from, watching the advance.

Lofter counted the three as they ran for the shelter but he could not know if there were others inside. Probably a cook at least, but in this working hour there should be no one idling indoors unless, hopefully, Sam Allee was there doing bookwork. He halted his crew behind the corral fence, cupped his hands, and bellowed.

"Hello, the house. All you in there come out with your hands up. We don't want to kill you but we will if you make a fight. Saddle up and clear off the place."

Wallie Martin eased his rifle through a corner of his window and threw a shot at Lofter. The bullet crashed into the top rail of the corral fence.

The Seven Rivers foreman jerked his horse around as a second shot whined toward him. Then he spurred back out of range, his crew opening fire to give him cover for the retreat even though their lead fell short of the log wall. Then all of them drew back into a tight group to assess what should be done.

Lofter was angry at the impasse. It had appeared a simple job to run off these intruders. To be held at bay this way by three or four men galled his pride.

It also brought Kid Diller's fury up. He was not accustomed to such frustration.

Diller snarled through clenched teeth, his jaw muscles bunched. "Rush them. Pump lead enough at those windows to drive them back, and we can get at them."

Hank Lofter spat his disgust. "We go in close enough for that we'll lose some boys. No need for that. Just sit tight until dark, then we can slip up and burn them out."

He dismounted and waved Diller down. After some hesitation the Kid shrugged and dropped out of his saddle. The rest followed, ground-hitched the animals, Lofter delegating the fresher men to keep watch. Then, with those who had ridden with him the day and night before, he stretched on the grassy knoll, dropped his hat over his face, and went to sleep.

The hardcases in the cabin understood the intention and were amused. Joe Gross made a tempting venture into the yard, drew an ineffective shot, and was delighted when the resting figures surged up to see what was happening. He laughed, waved a jaunty hand and leaned against the wall outside, knowing that Butch Rathbone and those with him cutting timber would have heard the firing and already be on their way down to investigate. It pleased him to see half the Seven Rivers crowd lie down again, not expecting any surprise.

It was only minutes until Rathbone's group eased down to the edge of the trees and sat looking out, studying the situation. Rathbone chuckled. "Spread out for a circle, boys, and we'll corral the jaspers before they know it."

The men moved apart, fanning into a skirmish line, then walked their horses into the open. The Seven Rivers crew's attention was all on the cabin, but facing them, Joe Gross saw his crew appear. Now his duty was to keep Seven Rivers occupied

with him as long as he could. For openers he raised
his rifle and shot, yelling at those inside to join him.
They jumped through the door and started forward,
firing even though there was no one within range to
hit.

Hank Lofter rolled up again, sat for a moment
watching, suspicious. Why would the idiots leave the
cabin and just waste ammunition? He swung to look
the other way. The sight of Rathbone's large party
sifting out of the trees jarred a curse from him, and
he lunged to his feet, sprinting for his horse, yelling
a warning. He made the animal, threw himself up
Indian fashion, low against the neck, and dashed off
the knoll between the cabin and the advancing riders. His men did not escape. Their rifles were
stacked army-style in one place; the horses were
grouped in another. Before they could run from one
to the other location they were trapped by the people in the yard on one side and Rathbone's headlong
charge on the other. Kid Diller and two others ran
but were ridden down, surrounded and forced back
to their group.

Seven Rivers, sullen and shocked, stood encircled
by Sam Allee's fighters. They had been sure their
force of twelve and their foreman would be more
than enough to overwhelm the few they expected to
find here. None of the other Park ranches kept
larger crews than six or seven riders. But counting
the four in the yard, there were twenty-five men
against them, men with the plain mark of hardcase
in their cold faces. And with rifles trained on them
like the inward-pointing spokes of a wheel.

Butch Rathbone's smile was ugly, his tone harsh.
"Drop your gun-belts and watch how you use your
hands."

Eleven of them unbuckled and let the belts fall.
Kid Diller did not move a muscle, glaring up from
close to Rathbone's horse. "To hell with you," he
snarled.

There was a frozen moment, then Diller slapped for his gun. Rathbone's boot pulled out of his stirrup and swung, caught Diller under the chin, lifted him off his feet, and flung him backward to the ground. Rathbone was on him in a leap from the saddle, landing astraddle, his big feet wide apart. He bent, snapped the gun from Diller's holster, tossed it toward the stacked rifles, stepped away and as the little killer tried to scramble up, flicked a gesture at him, then at his two closest riders. They hit the ground before Diller straightened, catching both his arms, holding him. He wrenched wildly, thrashing in his frenzied rage, blinded to consequences, but each rider was nearly twice his size. He kicked out at their legs. They stepped away, hands around his wrists, stretching his arms full length, yanking him off balance each time he swung a boot.

The four from the yard had come in on foot at an easy trot. Rathbone swept an arm around him, ordering the gun-belts gathered and taken with the stacked rifles to the cabin.

Joe Gross could not resist a jibe of mockery. "Thought you had us treed. Nice and easy, wasn't it? But it looks a little different now, I'd say."

No one answered. Seven Rivers stood stoic, a tough crew itself, one to one a match for those around them, waiting to hear what Rathbone intended doing with them.

The simple answer, Sam Allee's foreman thought, would be to shoot them now, but they were men of his own type, the kind he understood, and he shied away from wholesale slaughter as degrading to himself.

He said, "If I turn you loose, tell you to ride out, will you do it?"

Silence and stony stares were the only response. Rathbone tried again.

"I'll offer you just that chance. Move out of this Park as fast as your horses can take you. Don't go

back to the ranch for your plunder. Is that understood?"

No one broke. The guns covering them had not
cowed them. Rathbone cursed.

"You want it the hard way, all right. We'll start
by hanging one man, then see if you change your
minds. You want to draw lots?"

They did not. Rathbone looked at each of them in
turn as if unable to choose who would be the exam-
ple. Last, he turned to Diller.

"You'll do. Unless you want to get down on your
knees and beg."

Kid Diller spat at him.

Butch Rathbone bared his teeth. "You must be
crazy. Reese, Smith, bring rope and a horse."

One of his crew walked his animal to the Seven
Rivers mounts and led a black through the circle.
Another dismounted, used a thong to tie the wrists
Diller's holders forced behind him, then handed a
lariat to Rathbone. In dead quiet the foreman fash-
ioned a noose, tested that it ran free, slipped it over
one arm as he walked to Diller. With that hand he
grabbed a handful of hair as Diller jerked his head
from side to side, spitting again and again. With his
free hand he pushed the loop over the Kid's ears,
pulling it close around the neck. Diller was boosted
up on the horse and held there by his feet, still
trying to kick.

Those who had taken the guns to the cabin had
just run back, hurrying so they would not miss the
lynching. The circle of riders opened, the horse was
led through, escorted by four men, and the other
Seven Rivers captives were herded behind in a parade toward the timber. They were halfway there
when pounding hoofs drew their attention to the Allen road that came up from the south along the
creek. Sam Allee was spurring toward the party. He
hauled up in front of Rathbone at the head of the
column leading the Diller horse, his quick look tak-

ing in the bound Kid, the disarmed Seven Rivers crew afoot with most of Rathbone's men prodding them forward. His eyes came back to Rathbone.

"What's this, Butch?"

"Necktie party. Your brother made his first mistake."

"Good. But why hang Diller?"

"He talked back and spat on me. I picked him to spook this crowd into riding out of this country so far they'll never get back."

"No."

The big foreman reddened, swelled. "What do you mean, no?"

"Just that. You don't hang a man for those reasons. And I've got to live in this Park a long time. As soon as Drake is whipped your job is over and you'll be gone. I don't want my neighbors blaming me for hanging a man or men just for fighting for their outfit."

For a long moment Sam Allee thought Butch Rathbone would draw on him and shoot. He watched the man's struggle against his temper until the ice in his own eyes chilled the urge. Rathbone sat his horse, his fists clenched on his heavy thighs, his breathing loud, then he yanked the animal around and put it toward the cabin at a hard run.

The crew watched him go, amazed. They had never seen the foreman backed down until now. Allee faced them, rigid, his jaw tight for a full two minutes, in the grip of a cold, wicked anger. He hated Rathbone, hated all the man stood for. Hated himself for the need to resort to such tools to take what was rightfully his. The crew read the passion choking him but misunderstood it and made no move that might turn it on them.

Allee fought himself into control. When he could speak, he told Joe Gross, "Untie him. Get that damned rope off his neck."

Gross hesitated. He knew that Rathbone would

never forgive him, but looking at Allee's eyes he felt more in danger from Sam if he refused than he would be from the foreman. Rougher than need be he loosened the noose, dragged it over the Kid's head, then cut the thong off the wrists.

Allee said, "Diller, get out of here. Get out of the Park. Stay out."

The Kid's eyes smoked. "Captain," he said in a strangled voice, "I didn't ask you for help. I don't beg favors from any man."

"It wasn't for you, you cheap punk. Ride out while you can."

Diller sneered. "And you don't run me out of anywhere. You laid hands on me and I won't forget. When the chance comes I'll kill you."

There was insanity in the pale eyes. For an instant Allee regretted interfering here. There could be no question that Diller deserved hanging for past killings. But it was not in him to condone a lynching because of a man's loyalty.

Diller rode arrogantly to the Seven Rivers horses, changed from the one he was on to his own, and drove away through the deep grass. When he had gone, Allee focused on his brother's other riders.

"All of you too. Ride now before I change my mind."

One spoke stubbornly. "We need our guns."

"No guns. And if I catch you in North Park again, I'll let Rathbone have you."

Butch Rathbone had been right in one thing. The near hanging of Kid Diller convinced them riding out was the better choice. They rode, racing their horses until they were well out of rifle range.

Allee continued to face his fighting crew, feeling their displeasure with him. They had had a fight, they had won, they had captured Drake's men, and he had robbed them of their victory. He was not yet in control of his ranch. Drake would attack again with new riders. Sam still needed these. His job now was to make peace with his foreman.

He put his horse toward the cabin but had not reached it when a single rider appeared on the road coming in. At first he thought it was one of the Seven Rivers crowd returning, then he saw that it was a boy in overalls. He waited where he was until the horse pulled beside him and recognized Otto Schultz's son. He had not seen him in five years, but there was no mistaking the shock of almost white hair.

Fritz Schultz grinned, passing over a folded paper, saying, "Howdy, Sam. She told me to get it to you as quick as I could but when I got here they were shooting at each other so I hid in the brush until they were gone."

Allee read the note and forgot Butch Rathbone. Martha Bollen would not marry Drake. With blood suddenly hammering in his ears he told the boy, "Let's go. I'll ride back with you."

8

Sam Allee made the ride to Walden with impatient urgency, pushing his horse, hardly hearing Fritz Schultz's constant babble about fishing and hunting. For instance, there was his encounter with a bear the year before: he climbed a slender tree and perched there all day while the animal tried to shake him out, clawed the bark to ribbons trying to climb after him, and did not give up until dark. Pictures built in Sam's mind, of Drake somehow disposed of, of Martha Bollen settled in the fine new house he would build beside Moss Creek, of a life together with the eastern girl who had showed such awareness of the beauty and value of this land he loved.

Stopping before the hotel he brought himself back to reality enough to flip a dollar to the boy as he swung down, and to thank him for the errand. The towhead tossed it in his palm as if it were hot.

"You don't owe me, Sam. The lady already paid."

Sam's smile spread, wide and easy. "It's for my horse then. Take him in and rub him down good, but go easy on the water."

Fritz looked resentful, muttering that he knew his business as well as anyone. Sam paused the extra minute to assure him that he had forgotten for the moment that the boy had grown up, that he was sure he could trust in his judgment. Then he took the three steps to the porch in a single leap and sailed through to the lobby.

At the desk Achey Collins groaned, made shooing motions, with his hands, wailing, "Sam, go on back out quick, please. You'll be the ruin of me."

Sam Allee laughed at him, saying, "Relax, Achey. I just want to see Miss Bollen. Where is she?"

"She ain't here." It was said too quickly.

Sam waggled a finger close to the worried face. "You're a bad liar, friend. She sent me a note. What number is her room?"

Collins groaned again, rocking his head. "She's Drake's fiancée, Sam. He'd go wild if you went up to see her here. He'd burn me out sure."

Allee might have been amused at the man's fears except that he was in a hurry. He said rapidly, "Don't worry so, Achey. Drake hasn't got near the size crew he had. What room?"

Achey Collins' red tongue ran around his lips and as if it were a prayer he whispered, "Ten. But . . . ."

Sam Allee did not wait to hear what would follow

the *but*. He took the stairs in strong bounds, and his stride was long down the uncarpeted hall. He rapped a light tattoo on the door, humming without sound.

Her voice came, a breathless sound. "Who is it?"

"Sam. May I come in?"

"Oh." Relief made it a gasp. The key rattled in the lock inside, and the door was pulled open wide. "I was afraid it might be Drake. Sam, you're all right? You got my warning in time?"

He stepped through, closing the panel behind him, not bothering to correct her. "I came as soon as I got your message. How did you happen to hear him and Lofter? How did you get away from him?"

"I accidentally overheard them in his office. Then Lofter left and I went and faced Drake about his order. He told me it wasn't my business and not to interfere. Sam, I was so shocked. All I could do was watch for a chance, and when he rode off I tricked a boy into driving me to town with my luggage. I won't go back."

"Of course not. I'm sorry, Martha. It was a hard way to find out what he is, having been in love with him."

She shook her head almost fiercely. "I came out here to marry him and I'd have been a good wife if he'd been the man I thought he was. I'd have tried to love him. I hadn't begun to yet. There's a glamour about him that attracted all of us in St. Louis, something new to me, a rich rancher with miles of range and thousands of cattle. But now he's hateful."

Sam frowned, his brows drawing together. "You would have married for that reason, without love?"

"Of course." She sounded surprised. "Many women do and hope that love grows later. I needed security." As his frown deepened, irony touched her voice. "We don't have all the ways of solving problems open to men. Did you ever watch your father lose his last dollar buying stocks that turned out to be worthless? Were you ever wakened in the middle of the night to be told your father had shot himself? Were you ever thrown on the charity of your friends?"

At the last question he nodded quickly. "That, yes. When my father was killed, Drake got the ranch. I had to leave. A mountain tribe took me in. Now I understand." A deep flush rose hot in his face. "Martha, could you learn to love me? I think I've loved you since the moment I saw you get on that train."

She was silent, solemn for so long that coldness filled his stomach. Then she smiled, and the warmth of it brought a leap to his pulse; her words set it racing.

"Is that a proposal, Sam? You want to marry me?"

"Want to, yes. In a while. First I have to start my ranch, build you a decent house. Meanwhile, go back East and wait for me. Where Drake can't reach you and hurt you. He's perfectly capable of trying to beat you into submitting to him."

Fright made her pale. There had been time by now for Drake Allee to have learned from Link where she was and be on his way after her. She said weakly, "I haven't got train fare, anything left to live on."

He spun out of the door into the hall, pulled out his shirttail, and dug into his money belt. When he turned back into the room Martha Bollen was a stricken, drooping figure sunk on the chair beside the bed. She came up quickly, her hands against her face.

"I thought you'd left . . ."

He did not take time to explain, reaching for her hands, folding a packet of bills into them, talking rapidly: "It isn't much, only five hundred, about all I have now, but it will get you to St. Louis and carry you until you find something to keep you while I get a home ready."

Her fingers closed on the money briefly, then opened, and she held it toward him.

"All you have. Sam, I couldn't take that."

"Yes, you can. I won't really need it. Once I have my herd on government grass, the bank will loan me running expenses. Just write to me when you're settled."

He pushed the hands back against her throat, and touching her caused a sharp reaction. He had not intended the presumption of kissing her, but suddenly his arms were around her, his lips on hers, startling him more than it did the girl. For an instant she was passive; then she came alive, her body pressing hard against his.

He tore away, more shaken than he had ever been, and not daring to stay longer with her. Saying a quick good-bye, he bolted from the room, his thoughts whirling around her. Everything was breaking his way now. When he had the ranch established, when the house was built and furnished. When he could send for her . . ."

His mind was not on the street nor the people there as his long stride took him out of the hotel. He did not see the Seven River crew until it rushed out of the saloon behind him and the movement brought him around.

Kid Diller was with them, and the Kid was drunk. They caught Sam on the porch, two men pinning his arms before he could draw his gun. A third yanked it from his holster and threw it as far as the opposite sidewalk. The Kid pulled a knife from a neck sheath, crouching.

"Let him go." The tone was wicked, jubilant.

The men holding Sam jerked him off balance, flung him aside and jumped away. Diller's pointed tongue flicked out like a serpent's.

"You got a knife?"

Sam caught himself, straightened. "No."

The tongue flicked again. "Too bad. Too bad for

you. I'm going to carve my initials in you from head
to feet." He weaved in his crouch, thrusting the
knife point forward in front of him.

Sam Allee judged him coldly. In his years of wandering he had had to learn to fight in order to survive in barroom brawls. He had a quick confidence
in himself. He was bigger than Diller, heavier by
thirty pounds; there was more power in his strong
legs and arms. But unarmed against a knife . . . He
retreated four quick steps to put his back against the
hotel wall, shucking out of his coat, wrapping it
around his left arm.

Diller understood and charged recklessly to stop
him, slashing viciously at Sam's chest. Allee took the
thrust on the cloth-wrapped forearm. The blade
slashed into the fabric, but Sam's move deflected it
so that it only grazed the muscle. All Diller's weight
was behind the lunge, aimed to penetrate the breast-
bone, and the knife slid haft deep into the bulk of
the coat.

The stiff hand guards hooked in the weave. Too
late Diller tried to withdraw, wrenching back. The
knife did not pull free. While the Kid fought it,
Sam's right hand caught at the thin throat, fastened
tight on it, flung the body around so that his arm anchored beneath the chin. Arching, he hauled Diller's
head back, choking him.

The lighter man thrashed to break the grip. Allee
tightened it, lifting, until Diller's feet kicked in the
air above the floor. Sam had a second to sweep a
glance at the others on the porch.

In a half circle the Seven Rivers men watched intently. Each of them at one time or another had felt
the flash of Kid Diller's arrogant scorn. If you
worked for Drake Allee you walked shy of the little
killer. So they enjoyed this fight. It pleased them all
to see him taking the worst of it, watch the body
contact that he resented so.

Diller was resenting it, going wild. One kicking

foot hooked behind Sam Allee's leg and with that leverage Diller launched himself sideways, making Allee stumble. Another lurch to the side carried them both to the dusty, scarred floor, crashing against the row of chairs against the wall. The fall jarred loose Sam's grip on the neck, and Diller was quick to roll free, to twist to his feet with a cat-sure spring.

Allee was a second slower. Diller used the moment to wrench again at the knife, and this time it ripped out. By the time Sam's feet were set, the blade glittered, steady in the Kid's small hand. Diller jumped, thrusting, but Allee spun half away and one step back. Momentum carried Diller past him. As he lunged by, Sam grabbed the knife wrist in both hands, twisting savagely.

With a mad strength Diller kept his hold on the hilt until the wrenching broke his arm at the elbow. He shrieked a curse; his fingers spasmed open, and the knife flew out of them, clattered on the edge of the porch, and bounced off to the sidewalk. Allee was closer to the edge. He jumped the steps, scooped up the knife, and whirled with it toward the man diving down at him. Kid Diller tripped on the second step, fell forward, fell into the up-tilted point of the knife. It went through the base of his throat, was stopped only by the spine. Allee let go of the hilt, and Diller crumpled at his feet.

Sam Allee straightened, facing the half circle of men on the porch. Their attention was not on him. They were staring stupidly at the body on the ground, not believing what they saw. They began moving with slow steps as though Diller might spring up and attack them in furious mortification at being seen as the loser. Their eyes were hypnotized by the still figure. Allee drifted at the same pace along the porch edge, his lower body hidden by it. One rider ventured down the stairs, bent over the body and called without raising his head. "Dead. The Kid's dead."

Allee continued sidling without hurry, trying not to distract their attention from the thing that held them. He was just short of the mouth of the narrow alley at the side of the hotel when the drum of hooves made him look at the street behind him. Hank Lofter was there, riding down on him. Sam made the two long strides, turned into the alley, and ran.

The far end of the passage opened on the back lots of Walden, strewn with rubbish, old tin cans, shattered bottles, an open space broken only by a barn; but there was not time to reach that. The rear of the livery corral jutted out from the backs of the buildings a block away. He raced for the barn, ducked between the corral poles, dodged among the horses, and made it to the runway, hearing the chorus of shouts as the Seven Rivers riders reacted to Hank Lofter's cry of warning and started their chase down the alley.

Lofter was yelling: "Head him off. Cut around the hotel the other way. He'll try to double back for his gun."

Sam Allee wanted the gun, but this was not the time to go after it. Seven Rivers had not yet erupted baying out of the back of the alley; they had not seen where he turned. He pelted into the dim runway at his hardest run, panting, pausing where the towhead Fritz Schultz was forking hay into the feed trough of a box stall. They both heard the riders' spurs clang on the corral poles as they started through.

Sam gasped, "Can you get me out of sight before they're here?"

The boy had heard the hue and cry. He was quick-witted, pointing the fork. "Dive in the trough where I can cover you up."

Sam dived, wriggled under the hay already piled there. Fritz threw two quick forkfuls over him, then added more at a normal speed. It had a dusty, sweet smell and must be Big Blue, the stems longer than Gamma or Buffalo. It continued to fall, all but smothering him. Then he heard the muffled jangle of spurs on running boots and immediately Hank Lofter's thick voice.

"You, kid, where'd he go?"

There was a stupid note in Fritz's slow drawl. "Huh? Who?"

"Sam Allee. Didn't he run in here just now?"

"Nope." That was definite enough. "There's nobody been here the last hour."

Lofter swore. "Maybe he sneaked in and you didn't see him. Coolie, climb up in that mow with a fork, and spear through the hay. The rest of you, look in the office, in the other box stalls, see if he got out to the street."

The boots ran. Fritz Schultz continued tossing hay over Sam Allee until Sam thought there must be a mound high enough to give him away. He fought panic, fought against the sneezing that the dust in his nose was forcing, pinching the nostrils closed, breathing through his sleeve.

There was a long silence, then a voice echoed in the runway. "He ain't around here. He must not have come in at all."

9

Sam Allee lay listening, his leg muscles cramping with his tension, but he did not dare to move. The silence did not relieve him. It could be a portent that someone had wondered at the excess of hay in this one particular trough, that Hank Lofter was gloating, putting out a hand to receive a long-tined fork. At any second it could be jammed through the dry grass to spit him through and pin him to the wooden box. Sam had a flash of the trough as his coffin. To loosen his frozen mind he counted. It was a long, long five minutes before a soft voice close above him said, "All right. They went down the street, into the hotel. I watched them all the way. And I looked clear around the livery."

Sam Allee swam up through the hay, sitting, twisting to ease his legs as sharp needles tingled through them. An involuntary sneeze caught him unaware before he could more than clamp a hand over his nose and mouth. He used his handkerchief, blew into it hard. With his throat still clogged, his voice was choked.

"Fritz, this is twice today I owe you. I won't forget. Do you have a gun I can borrow?"

The fourteen-year-old's grin was wide as though throwing Seven Rivers off the scent was some sort of game he had enjoyed. He bobbed his head.

"Pa's is hanging in the office. I'll fetch it."

While he was gone Sam Allee climbed out of the trough, stamped the circulation back into his feet, combed hay out of his hair and off his face with his clawed fingers, beat at his clothes, coughed the dust from his throat until he could breathe normally.

Fritz came back, handed over the gun, saying, "You want me to saddle your horse or you staying here?" He fished a handful of ammunition from a pocket and dropped it in Sam's palm.

"Saddle him."

The boy went for the animal. Sam examined the gun. It was old, a single action forty-five, almost an antique, but it was oiled and appeared in working order. He filled the chamber, tucked it under his belt buckle, and walked toward the rear door where Fritz was tightening the cinch. As the boy straightened Sam put a dollar in his hand, smiling.

"Thanks again. Now take a walk, go buy a soda at Grosmer's."

This time the towhead took the money with a saucy flip of his shoulders and swaggered toward the front entrance. Sam watched until he had angled across the street out of sight. He was taking a chance in leaving the barn in daylight, but he did not want either himself or the boy there if Seven Rivers decided Allee had been there after all and came back. There was no telling what the crew might do to the boy if they thought he had hidden Sam, and he was not going to take the chance of their finding out.

He untied the horse, swung up, settled himself in the saddle, took up the reins. Then suddenly he jammed his spurs deep. The animal exploded through the rear of the runway. Allee drove past the corral, across the open fields, heading for the isolated barn at the edge of the rolling, uncut grasslands of the Park. If Seven Rivers was in the hotel saloon, they would not see him; and if he knew the type, they would have repaired there to decide where to look next.

He almost made it. Then a gun flashed from the barn corner, hit the horse in the neck. The animal went down in a running, twisting fall. Sam Allee kicked out of the stirrups just before they touched ground, landed on his feet, and was propelled on at a staggering lope that saved his life. A second shot missed him. He pulled the antique gun, leveled a shot at the last powder flash, and was startled when a man was flung sideways into sight.

Allee did not wait to see more. There could be others waiting there in ambush. He spun, made a dashing retreat to the livery as the closest shelter. Shouts from the street beyond told him the shots had been heard as he dived back into the runway and stopped in a crouch to drag a breath and shove another bullet into the forty-five. He knew he could not stay there, could not again successfully hide in the stall.

A wild look around showed him the ladder up to the mow above. He jumped and climbed. The mow was better than half-filled with loose hay. He could burrow into that, but it would now surely be searched again, and he did not want a hay fork through his back.

But the rear door of the mow above the runway was open. The wide fork on the pulley by which hay was lifted up from a wagon dangled there. He waded the hay in lunging strides, caught the pulley rope, hauled himself up until he straddled the top of the fork, then reached for the edge of the livery roof. Perversely the fork swung in a circle. His arm stretched to its utmost before he steadied the rope, took a solid grip on the roof, and shinnied up the pulley rope, clawed over the eaves, and rolled onto the roof.

Because of the heavy winter snow load the roof was steeply pitched, but a high false front hid it from the street. Sam Allee lay where he was, recovering his breath. Then he worked closer to the front where he would be less visible from the back of the barn and not visible at all from the street; he lay there on his stomach.

It had been a long day. After the confrontation with Butch Rathbone, the ride to Walden, the fight with Kid Diller, he felt close to exhaustion. The temptation was to give in to it, to go to sleep. But he must not. He looked toward the west. The fading sun would be behind the Medicine Bows within minutes, twilight here was very short. If he were not discovered before dark, he just might escape.

He rested with his chin on his crossed arms, listening. Twice he nearly dozed off but the sounds that came up roused him both times. The street was full of the noisy curious. The barn echoed with voices. His brother's crew was searching there more thoroughly, then searching the mow, probing it foot by foot with forks, calling to each other. By the voices Sam could place where the men were, and they had not yet reached the opening of the mow.

Hank Lofter's roars dominated the rest. The foreman was beside himself with frustration. A man did not vanish into thin air. No one on the street admitted having seen the missing Allee. He had to be in the barn, and the tightened search ate up time.

It was dark outside before anyone thought of the roof. And at dark Allee slithered to the ridge of the steep pitch, where he could see the buildings paralleling the street. On his left was the open area of the corral. There was no place to go in that direction. Neither could he make the long drop to the street over the false front; that would take him into the arms of the men hunting him. He could not get away by the rear, for they were back there now yelling for ladders.

But on his right was a small building where a doctor and two lawyers kept offices. It was only half the length of the barn, its shed roof sloping from front to back, and it was separated from the barn by a four-foot gap. Allee skidded down to the eaves, rose to a crouch, and with the sharp slant to shove against, launched himself across. His boots made his landing loud. He only hoped the sound was covered by the noises at ground level.

Then the clatter of wood on wood signaled that a ladder was being set against the barn roof and someone would soon be coming up it. He had to go somewhere and go fast. The only possible shelter was the stone chimney jutting through the center of the roof he was on, and he sprinted for that, huddling down on its far side. From there he heard men on the barn, the scrape of their boots as they climbed to the ridge, the short, shocked silence of another disappointment, and curses called down.

"He ain't here either. Where the hell . . .?"

In the new darkness Sam Allee risked putting his head out around the chimney corner, only far enough so that if it were seen, it could be mistaken for one of the round river rocks that gave the masonry a lumpy outline. He saw shadowy figures moving on the ridge across the gap, staying up there as if he would somehow appear. He drew the forty-five, concerned that they might decide to jump and look at his hiding place, although he knew that he would be discovered if he had to fire. One man did slide down and look over the edge of the eaves into the gap, then apparently chose not to try a leap. In the dim early starlight Sam could make out the movement as the man turned to scramble back up; then there was a blur of flailing arms, a high yell, and the figure slipped backward off the roof, fell to the ground and screamed.

He had not been killed, but the accident attracted attention off the search for the moment. The second man on the barn disappeared down the far side of the roof. Others ran into the gap, someone carrying the livery lantern to show the injured one. But there would be no safety for Sam Allee in staying where he was.

Beyond this building rose the three-story hotel. The separation between them was only three feet. There were no lighted windows on the second floor and on the third only the one at the back corner. It was also the only one with the sash raised, the shade drawn half down and showing bright points and fingers through holes and splits in the fabric. Hoping that anyone who had been in back of the buildings had gone to investigate the fall, Sam ran in a low crouch down the slanting roof to the corner. He knew that a drainpipe ran down there from the hotel roof, held against the wall by heavy brackets. If they would support his weight, he could climb. Standing at the edge of the roof, he leaned across, spread one palm on the hotel wall, felt for the pipe, located one bracket at his head height, and pulled down hard on it. It seemed secure, but if he trusted it and it gave way, he would fall. The drop was only seven feet here, of itself not too dangerous. The danger would come if he landed on litter, crashed on cans and bottles that would make a loud noise. There was too much chance of running afoul of the pursuers on the ground.

Yet there was no choice left. Allee stretched one foot over, fumbled for a lower bracket, tested his weight on that, and when it held, took the higher one in both hands, lifting. They were set about a foot apart. He went up overhand, his arms taking the burden, his feet having little leverage on the thin rims of the strap iron encircling the pipe.

When his head was a little above the level of the open sash he reached the two feet across to it, tightened his fingers over the sill, and leaned to look in at the room. He did not know who was there or if the lamp had been left for the occupant's return, but it would not be one of the Seven River Crew. They could have been looking down on him all this while, and he wondered that they had not thought of this logical location for surveying the lower roofs.

He saw a woman in a chair beside the little table where the lamp stood, a blonde head bent over a book, and in a rush of relief recognized Martha Bollen. Afraid she would scream if he startled her, he whispered her name very softly, then again a trifle louder. At his fourth call the head lifted, tilted on one side.

"It's Sam Allee, Martha," he said. "Outside your window. Turn out the lamp so I can come in without being spotted. My brother's crew is after my scalp."

The girl came to her feet in a rush, turning, letting the book drop unnoticed, her eyes wide, staring at the window. Only a hand clawing at the sill was visi-

ble. Allee had pulled back where he was not silhouetted against the lighted rectangle. She came against
the wall, bent to look outside, and found his face a
foot from hers. Gasping at what appeared a very
precarious hold on a fragile support, Martha Bollen
drew her head back, went to the lamp, and blew out
the yellow flame.

Sam Allee inched himself higher, clamped his
knees around the pipe, let go of it with his hand, and
reached quickly for the sill. His first grab missed.
His knees slipped down, their grip loosened by
his twisted position. He stretched his arm again, but
now the fingers would not reach the window frame.
He snatched for the pipe again, caught it, his muscles quivering, and clung like a monkey, gathering
himself for another try. It would be deepest irony if
he did not have the strength left to make it into the
room now.

He had to let go of the sill to shinny higher. He
heard the girl's sharp intake of breath. Then her
head came through the opening, bent to look toward
the ground.

"I'm still here," he told her sardonically. "Be
there in a minute. I hope."

Knowing that he could not hang for long, Sam Allee put extra effort into working up the pipe until he
could reach down to the sill, then leaned to tighten
his fingers over it. A touch surprised him. The girl
wrapped both her hands around his wrist, squeezing
hard. She could not hold him if he slipped, but the
thought brought a surge of exultation, the spur he
needed to make the next necessary move. This time
his knees held; his second hand reached the sill and
grappled it. Gritting his teeth until his jaws bulged,
he swung free, heaved his body toward the window,
lifting with the last of his power. The lunge took his
head and chest through the opening but he would
have fallen back except for the girl. Butting into her,
he knocked her backward, still clinging to his wrist,

and her fall, sudden and heavy, pulled him with her far enough so that his rib cage dragged over the frame. From there, hauling on her arms, he wriggled the rest of the way until his knees doubled and dropped him on the floor.

While he panted and trembled, recovering slowly from the savage call on his energy, Martha Bollen twisted from under the exhausted body, got to her feet, pulled the cracked shade full down, then put a match to the lamp wick. As the glow spread, she had her first clear sight of Sam Allee where he lay rolling slowly from stomach to back. His shirt was torn, ripped at the sleeve seams from the extreme stretching. One trouser leg was gashed where a spur had slashed it in the fall from his horse. The clothes were stained with dirt from the pipe, stems of hay still clinging to them, and one sleeve was blood-soaked from the graze of Kid Diller's knife.

Her voice came in a rising wail. "Sam Allee, whatever has happened to you?"

"Fight. Chase." It was all he had the breath to say.

"Your arm. Were you shot?"

"Knife. Not bad." After a pause he added, "Do you have a drink of water here?"

She pivoted toward the washstand, and he heard the lip of a pitcher clatter against the rim of a thick glass. When she crossed the room again Sam had shoved up and back on his buttocks to half-sit, half-lie against the wall. She held the glass to his lips, tipping it for short sips until he had emptied it and asked for more. She was pouring again when a rapid knocking rattled the door. Sam tried but he could not get up. He groaned half aloud, wrenched the old forty-five out of his belt, and straightened against the wall spread-legged, steadying the gun on his thigh.

"Miss Bollen." It was Achey Collins' low, nervous whine. "Marshal Gunnison and Hank Lofter, they're right downstairs searching for Sam Allee. I didn't tell them about you. You got to leave before they see you here. Quick, while they're going through the second floor. I'll get you past them when they look in the back rooms."

The rattling continued insistently. Martha Bollen raised her brows at Sam, crossing to whisper, "Are you able? Can we do it?"

Allee clenched his teeth, got his knees under him, but his lower legs would not hold him up. He whispered back, "You go. When I hear them up here I'll try a jump for the next roof." He did not believe the legs would recover in that time, but he was not going to involve her here with him. If Lofter found them together he would report to Drake and what jealous vengeance his brother would take against her would surely be vicious.

But the blonde had a fiber developed through the years of her own fight to survive.

Achey Collins called again, urgent. "Hurry. Hurry, Miss."

She answered loudly. "I will do nothing of the kind. I am in bed. You tell Lofter there is a lady retired in here and he is not to break in on me."

The door rattled harder, the knob turned sharply, but the bolt had been thrown, and the panel remained closed. Collins kept pleading more and more desperately as the long minutes dragged out.

10

Sam Allee rested against the wall until he heard the hollow tramp of boots on the stairs at the far end of the uncarpeted hall. Then by force of will, holding onto the chair Martha Bollen brought, he pulled himself upright. He stood for some seconds; then his knees collapsed and he went down on them.

Martha Bollen waited no longer. Against his ear she hissed, "Crawl under the bed."

"First place they'll look."

"I'll see they don't."

Without waiting for more argument the girl began throwing off her clothes, first the shoes and stockings, then the long dress, began untying the ruffled petticoat below the lace-trimmed chemise. Sam Allee let the ghost of a smile come. It might work. Even Hank Lofter should hesitate to search a room where the girl he thought his boss would soon marry lay in bed, for Drake's retaliation would be brutal. On knees and elbows he crawled to the low, sagging bed, lay flat, and wriggled beneath it, back to the wall it stood against.

He could see her bare feet hurry to the chair. She moved it to the bedside, tumbled the dress across the seat; then the rest of her garments dropped in a deliberately careless pile on the floor, thus hiding the underside of the bed. A moment later the hem of a long, half-transparent nightgown fell to her ankles. The springs sagged further, almost touching Allee's shoulder, as she climbed under the covers and flounced around, tossing them into disarray.

Achey Collins had fallen into an ominous silence. His feet beat a hurried retreat. Shortly there was a heavier knock, the door was tried, a gruff voice commanded it be opened.

"This is Marshal Gunnison. There's a killer loose in town we have to find."

The springs creaked. Martha Bollen's bare feet padded across, the key was turned in the lock, the bolt thrown back, and she pulled the door wide, one hand on it, one on the jamb. Her voice was chilling.

"You won't find him or anyone else with me, I assure you."

Sam Allee heard two grunts as though the air had been driven out of Gunnison and Lofter by body blows. Then Lofter's choked gasp: "Miss Bollen. You here? What the. . . .?"

Gunnison's rumble of apology overrode the foreman's strangled words. "Ma'am, we're sorry. Of course he wouldn't be here."

Martha Bollen began to close the door but suddenly Lofter stepped forward, set his foot against the bottom.

"Something's wrong here, Marshal. I'm going to have a look."

"No you are not," Gunnison barked. "Obviously the lady was in bed and wouldn't have a strange man with her."

"I'm not sure he is a stranger. First time I saw her she was with Sam Allee." Lofter's voice was strong with suspicion.

Gunnison's quick anger crackled. "I saw that. Don't insult her. They came in on the same stage, and he helped with her baggage. Clear out of here, Hank."

But Lofter was dogged. "Not until I'm sure he's not in there."

Martha Bollen's laugh was brittle. "Mr. Lofter, I am in only my nightdress. Drake Allee will have something to say to this outrage."

Under the bed Sam Allee held the old gun ready in case Lofter indeed dared look beneath the bed.

There was a short hesitation, then the marshal's threat: "I think he will. And if you make one more move, I will arrest you for harassment of a lady."

Lofter did not make the last move that would have won him a bullet between his eyes. Allee was prepared to shoot and take his chances with the marshal later, but Gunnison's tone was so cold, so deadly that the foreman quit. They left, the marshal apologizing to the girl until the door was closed. Martha locked it, bolted it, and crossed toward the bed just as Sam wriggled from under it. She started to speak, stopped as he pressed a finger against his mouth, pointing another at the door. Her blue eyes widened, darkened with awareness that Lofter could still be outside, listening for voices.

Allee lay on the floor ready to roll out of sight again at the first sign that the foreman was lingering, but minutes passed and no sound came through the thin wall. Martha Bollen used the time riffling through her bags, finding a frilly, long-sleeved robe, drawing it over her gown, tying the ribbon at her waist. Then she sat down on the cluttered chair, watching Sam in troubled silence.

Sam had decided the men actually were gone and was getting up, had lifted himself far enough to sit on the edge of the bed before he tried a final push to his feet. Again knuckles rapped on the door, lightly. Sam slipped back to the floor.

Martha called sharply. "What is it now? Who's there?"

Allee thought it would be Achey Collins, there to continue urging the blonde to leave. Instead a feminine voice answered: "Milly Wertz. Please let me come in. It's important."

Martha raised inquiring brows to Sam and he nodded. "A girl I've known most of my life." He whispered it. "She's all right. If she's alone. Give me a minute."

He pulled up to the bed, then to his feet, and now he could stand on them without support though the muscles still quaked. With the old revolver in his hand he tiptoed to the door, put his back against the wall next to it where the panel when it opened would shield him in case Lofter were forcing Milly to get him in. Then he signaled to Martha. The blonde stood up, padded across, unlocked, and opened, swinging the door and jumping away out of reach. Milly saw her from the hall, froze for a second, then came through stiff-legged, her back rigid, pushed the door shut behind her, discovered Sam out of the corner of her eye, snapped a glance from the girl in the filmy robe to the tumbled bed, then to Allee, and her face colored. Then she saw the gun in his hand, and she opened her mouth to speak but cut the words off as he frowned and shook his head.

He mouthed the question without sound. "Are Lofter or Gunnison in the hall?"

Her voice was flat, chilly. "No. They went out of the hotel just as I was coming toward it. Why?"

Allee shoved the gun under his belt, his mouth twisting. "They searched the place for me. Milly, meet Martha Bollen who put on the act of a lady gotten out of bed, indignant and refusing to let them look through her room. I was on the floor underneath there."

Some of the starch went out of the mountain redhead. She acknowledged the introduction with a brusk dip of a nod, but the green eyes showed suspicion that the story was a quick fabrication to explain the scene she had walked in on. Without looking again at Martha she said, "Isn't this the woman I heard had come to marry Drake? Why would she help you?"

"She changed her mind when she overheard him tell Lofter to run me out or kill me; then, when she charged him, he told her it wasn't her business. She came to town and sent me a warning. That's why I'm in Walden. Now, what brought you?"

"Good of her." Milly was still frosty. "I've got another warning. I rode in to check the title to the old Kings Canyon mine. A pair of strangers went up there poking around until Tom's boys sent them packing. Rob and I got talking that maybe we should file on it to make sure nobody else tried it. Sam, what's the road brand on the herd you're bringing in?"

Uneasiness made Allee short. "Flying A, but what's that got to do with the mine?"

"You sure I can talk in front of her?"

"I'm sure." Sam was impatient with Milly's delay, his concern growing though he did not know what she was getting at.

"I suspected that. Ephraim Dole, the county clerk, is an old friend of ours and opened the office after hours for me as a favor. I was back in the stacks looking through the books to see if the mine was clear of claims when another stranger came to the office. I heard him say he wanted to register a brand. Ephraim said he'd have to come back during office hours but the man told him he'd come clear from Cowdry and didn't know when he could get in again, and that he had a trail herd coming down from Nebraska any day. So Ephraim made the registration. For Flying A. When the man left I looked. The name he used was Hinkle Rathbone. Do you know him?"

Sam Allee's stomach knotted to a cold, sinking weight, and his voice was bitter. "Foreman of the crew I brought to fight Drake with. So he means to steal my cattle now."

Martha Bollen spoke for the first time since Milly

had arrived, a plaintive question. "Why would he do that? How could he?"

"Because I faced him down today in front of his men. And how is simple. With Flying A registered to him who's to say he doesn't own the herd?"

"Why, you will, certainly."

"If I stay alive, yes."

The blonde kept a sudden, shocked silence for a second, then almost inaudibly said, "Such awful, awful people there are in this place. Drake and his murderers after you on one side and your own men turning against you on the other. Sam, you haven't a chance now."

Allee sounded doggedly stubborn. "We'll see. Milly, how did you know to find me here?"

The green eyes were as concerned as Martha's blue ones. "I knew I had to reach you as fast as possible. I asked Fritz at the livery if he'd seen you. He said you'd come to town to see . . . her . . . at the hotel. I had to threaten Achey Collins to get the room number. But now you're cooped up with Seven Rivers hunting for you, is there anything more I can do?"

"You can get me a horse. Mine was shot." Allee spoke tightly.

The redhead's eyes closed to narrow slits, and her voice was thoughtful. "If Seven Rivers is watching the livery and I go there for one, they're going to wonder what happened to the one I rode to town. But mine's at the courthouse hitch rail. If you can get there."

"No, Milly, that would put you in danger."

"Not if I just stay around here until Drake's goons give up and leave Walden. It's the best way."

"Well, I guess so," he said uncertainly.

Listening to the mountain girl Martha Bollen heard in the urgent tone something more than a simple readiness to help a friend, but her first interest was in how Sam Allee thought he could move from this room all the way to the isolated courthouse, and she asked.

He smiled a reassurance, took both her hands and explained. "We turn out the lamps here and in the hall, then I can go out the back window to the kitchen roof, drop off, and circle out through the dark. Don't worry."

But there was deep worry in her upturned face and her voice. "Oh, do be very careful, Sam."

He nodded, squeezing the hands. "Turn the lamp out now. Milly, will you get the one in the hall, then see if there's anybody moving around out back?"

Milly Wertz was gone for some minutes. Standing beside the door in the dark room Sam Allee wanted to take Martha in his arms, carry with him the scent of her, but he did not want the mountain girl to surprise them and possibly embarrass the blonde easterner. In the drawn out silence he heard the squeal of the pulleys as a window sash was raised.

Then after a delay Milly slipped into the room again, saying softly. "Everything is quiet. I went down the kitchen roof and had a long look. I don't think anyone is watching, or I'd have been challenged."

He told her roughly, "You took a chance, you could have been shot . . . Thanks for everything."

Then he was gone. His soft footfalls receded down the hall. After that there was no further sound. Milly Wertz gave him time to be on the ground and away, holding her breath, only letting it out in a deep sigh when no shot had broken the night.

"Now light your lamp again, ma'am, while I light the hall one in case Achey Collins comes snooping up here."

She went back to the hall window, closed and locked that and put a match to the wick of the lamp in the hall bracket, then returned to the room. The eastern girl was standing by the table. She watched Milly narrowly as she came in, closed and locked the door, then faced the blonde across the room, her expression deliberately empty.

Martha Bollen said abruptly, "How close are you and Sam Allee, child?"

One corner of Milly's mouth quirked up in annoyance at the inference against her age. She said tonelessly, "I've known him for years. Why?"

"Your families were friends?"

The redhead's laugh was harsh. "Like hell. Sam is the only Allee we'd ever let come up the canyon. My pa and Sam's hated each other, but mine took a shine to Sam and let him stay with us when Drake drove him off Seven Rivers, practically raised him anyhow. Now how close do you think you are to him? Are you trying to marry him now you've run out on Drake?"

Martha Bollen caught her breath at the scorn in the other's tone, then she controlled the rise of anger and said in a careful voice, "I haven't decided yet."

"I have. When I was ten. My mind hasn't changed."

Startled, the eastern girl's brows rode up, and she laughed at the ridiculous idea. "What does Sam say to that?"

"I haven't told him."

"Then don't set your heart on him. Men most often make their own choices. You'll learn that as you grow up."

Milly's chin lifted in defiance. "Oh, I know you're a pretty lady with fancy clothes and fine manners, but it won't make any difference what you do. I am going to marry him. Good night."

Milly Wertz let herself out of the room, closing the door firmly but quietly behind her. Martha heard her boot heels march down the corridor, then drop with light confidence down the stairs. Again she wanted to laugh. Then she did not. There was something very convincing about the little mountain girl.

11

Sam Allee would have been bewildered to hear the opening of a fight over him, but his mind was not now on either girl. It had been concerned with reaching the horse at the courthouse, with making the escape from Walden; once he was sure of that, his concentration returned to the Flying A.

A burning rage at Butch Rathbone and his riders cauterized his being. All his experience had been in a school dominated by the belief that a ranch hand must be loyal to his outfit no matter what. The treachery of Rathbone plotting to steal his cattle and probably the land on which he intended to build his spread while still drawing wages from him was hardly possible to comprehend. He did not know what they planned, but certainly they were aware that a takeover could not succeed as long as he was alive. So he must move first, ride to the Allen ranch, and learn what he could there without being discovered.

Late as it was by the time he approached the place he saw light within the original headquarters building. They were awake then, likely celebrating the registering of his brand in Rathbone's name. There were no dogs to raise an alarm so he should be able to slip in, listen below the window.

He tied the horse in a draw some hundred feet from the house and moved on afoot through the light of the waning moon, reached the front wall, and stood close beside the open window. Rathbone's heavy laugh, his gloating voice came clearly.

"Like taking candy from a baby, boys. We play along until the herd gets here, drygulch Allee before he guesses a thing, send the trail crew packing, and we've got a ranch. We run out the brother's crowd and take Seven Rivers too. That's a lot to come by for nothing but a little scrap, ain't it?"

Sam Allee was so intent on trying to hear the reactions, to learn if any one of the men would protest the disloyalty and might be counted as an ally that he did not see the one who stepped out through the door behind him and paused to roll a smoke, did not know anyone was there until the yell came.

"Hey. Who's that by the window?"

Inside there was a momentary silence, then an explosion of sounds as chairs scraped back and the whole crew rushed for the door. Sam Allee did not wait for them to erupt through it. He snapped a shot at the man who had yelled, saw him dodge around the corner of the building without returning the fire, probably because he wore no gun at the moment.

That gave Sam time, a very short time, to make a dash for Milly Wertz's horse, and he used the time hard, running, not wasting a second in looking over his shoulder. Behind him the crew was clumsy in getting outside; then in a straggle they were yelling, baying after him. A gun went off. Lead kicked dirt beside one driving foot. More firing followed as he raced a weaving course to spoil an aim. He was not hit. They were using short guns. Apparently in their haste no one had thought to bring a rifle, and the reach of the forty-fives was not accurate enough to find him.

At the lip of the draw he jumped, landed halfway down the bank, and jumped again. The firing stopped suddenly, and a third leap took him to the animal. He yanked the picket line loose, swung up, drove his spurs deep, and they lunged up the far bank. In the depression he had been out of sight but on top he was again in the open and flung around in the saddle to see where the pursuit was. They had turned back to the corral for their animals, giving him another spate of time while they scrambled to saddle.

He set off across the grassland at a run, debating what direction to take. There were no friends he could go to, certainly none at Seven Rivers headquarters, none in Walden except Martha Bollen, and he could not turn to her for help again without endangering her. He felt a man alone under the wide, pale arch of sky, a vulnerable target for the men who would soon be on his trail, a man with nowhere to hide. And their horses would be fresher than the one that had already carried him here from Walden.

There was nowhere for him except possibly Kings Canyon. He had been told emphatically not to go there again. The only person in the hills who might befriend him was Milly Wertz, who at least had taken the trouble to warn him about Rathbone. She would understand how alone he was. But could she persuade her relatives to give him a temporary base, not turn him back to the mercies of his cutthroat crew?

If she were home yet. He did not know how long she had remained in Walden or whether she might still be there. Yet it was his last option, the only way open to him. He turned the horse toward Cowdry and as if it knew that was the direction toward home, it lengthened its stride.

As he struck the Encampment road and turned toward the little post office lunchroom the sounds of the pursuit were growing louder in the quiet night. Allee still had a mile lead, but the fresher horses were closing it. If they turned into the road in the same direction he took he would be run down before he reached the timbered canyonside.

Driving the animal as hard as he dared he said a

silent prayer that he would not ride into the Seven Rivers crew heading home from Walden. That would be all he needed, to be caught sandwiched between them and Rathbone. But he had met no one by the time he raised the cluster of Cowdry, surprised to see a light in the lunchroom. Passing it, another surprise was the horse tethered at the rail. He hauled up, swinging closer cautiously, looking for a brand that could read Seven Rivers, then breathed in sharp relief. In the light from the door he saw the mark on the shoulder, the simple S that Otto Schultz burned on the animals he reserved for rental.

It flashed on him that the towheaded Fritz could be here, that this animal must be fresher than the one he was on. He might switch, might even borrow a rifle from Emma Devers. It would cost precious minutes, but a new mount could save him and some gun other than the old forty-five he had borrowed would give him equal range with those chasing him.

He jumped his horse in beside the other, flung off, dropped the rein over the rail, and vaulted to the porch. Opening the door he stopped in mid-stride. Milly Wertz sat at the counter gossiping with Mrs. Devers over coffee.

The redhead pivoted to the door as it opened, saw Allee, and gasped. "What are you . . ."

He cut her short. "My crew's after me. I need a gun, another horse." He ran toward the rifle across the deer hoofs on the side wall, reached it down. "Shells."

Emma Devers had lived in this country all her life, remembered well the Indian scares of twenty years before. Without question she reached beneath the counter, came up with a box of thirty-thirty cartridges, and shoved them toward him. Allee spilled them in a pocket, levered the chamber full, talking as he worked.

"Milly, your horse is about winded. Let me take the rental. They're coming fast."

She was on her feet already. "Where you headed?"

"The canyon. Only place I can go."

"I'll come with you."

"No. They'd run us down."

She called over her shoulder on her way to the door. "You need me to get in there. Take Otto's nag and I'll ride Ginger. I'm lighter than you."

There was no time to stand and argue. He was on her heels across the porch, swinging up as she did, carrying the rifle in his left hand because there was no boot. Even as they drove away from the rail the drum of hooves was loud. The pursuit was dangerously close.

The trail north was now upgrade, slowing them, but it would also slow Rathbone's crowd. From the way they had been overtaking him Sam knew they had driven their mounts full out, trying to catch him before he made the rough country with the heavy pole pine and aspen growth. It would be touch and go whether he and the girl could stay ahead that far, get into the brush and trees that kept the moonlight out. There they might have some chance of making a stand.

It was eight miles from Cowdry to the mouth of Kings Canyon. They had covered only a quarter of the distance when Milly's horse faltered a good length ahead of him. With a sinking in his stomach he knew they could not go further.

The girl knew too. She reined in until he caught up, calling quickly, "We can make the first brush. Pull off in it until they pass, then cross the creek, and circle up, but don't show yourself until I've seen the family."

"Leave you?" The words came shocked.

"They won't bother me. They're hell-bent after you."

"They'll think you're me and shoot you."

"No. I'll pull off too, leave Ginger at the roadside,

and wait in the brush. When they see her and pull up, I'll call, ask why they're chasing me. That will throw them off your trail." She urged the tired animal on, nursing its failing strength.

Sam Allee groaned. There was no alternative to her plan. If they stayed together and were caught, he would be shot or hanged, and they could not let the girl live to stand as a witness to the murder. Outlaws such as these would not hesitate to kill a woman who was a threat to them. He rode on at her side.

She chose the place for their parting, another half mile ahead at a bend in the road banked by a stand of pine so dense that he had to get down, break the lower dead branches to make a path for the horse. Here he was in heavy shadow. Feeling his way, counting steps, he moved twenty feet before he heard the pound of hooves on the road and stopped, holding one hand over the animal's nose.

Shortly they drummed by. Allee judged that the girl had had time to ride only another hundred or so feet before she too worked back out of sight. As soon as they were past him he led his animal back through the path he had broken, to the edge of the road, confident that the noise the crew was making and the soft bed of needles underfoot covered any sounds he made. He must make certain that no harm came to Milly Wertz, for suddenly, without considering why, he knew that her well-being was more important to him than his own safety.

At the road he left the horse, eased forward to see around the bend, stopped just short of moving into sight, for the moonlight showed him Butch Rathbone and his outlaws pulled up around a riderless horse standing head down, heaving.

Rathbone's hoarse, triumphant shout was vicious. "Come out here, you. You ain't been off that animal long enough to be far. We'll hear you if you move, and if you stay put until daylight we'll dig you out."

There was silence. Rathbone shouted again.

This time a quavering voice answered, Milly's voice. "What do you want with me?"

Rathbone cursed. "A woman? What you doing in there?"

"I heard you chasing me. I was frightened."

"Naw." It was a harsh laugh. "We ain't after you. Just come out where we can see you."

There was the sound of crackling brush. A lantern was lit. Milly Wertz stepped into its yellow glow, a shrinking, unsure small figure.

Rathbone bellowed at her. "Where's that Sam Allee?"

She quavered, "Who?"

He swore at her. "Don't give me that act. You live in these parts, you know him, and he was on this road just minutes ago, same time as you. What you doing here if you wasn't with him?"

Her voice sharpened. "Mister, I don't know who you are or what business it is of yours. I was in Walden last evening. I stopped at Cowdry for coffee on my way home."

He turned sardonic. "Where is this home? Laramie?"

"Kings Canyon. Just above here."

None of the riders knew this country, and one cut in. "Hell with her, Butch. Every minute we waste here he gets further ahead. Let's ride."

Rathbone growled anger at him, then agreed in an impatient rasp. "Maybe. Petrie, you stay here with this female. Don't let her get away. I still think she knows where Allee is and is pulling a fast one on us."

Petrie was a big man with a small voice. "She's got red hair and green eyes and a gun on her hip."

"Take it away from her."

From his place in the shadow Sam Allee saw the crew's guns drawn and trained on the girl carelessly.

Petrie spat in the dust. "No offense, ma'am. Let's have the little toy before somebody gets hurt."

Allee saw her hesitate, knew she hated to surrender the gun, but she had no choice. She pulled the thirty-two gingerly and passed it to the man.

Petrie looked at it lying in his huge palm and laughed. "Regular cannon, ain't it though." He shoved it into a trousers pocket as Rathbone swung an arm and took the crew up the road at a run. "Honey, fetch us a little wood to keep the bears away. A fire never hurts on a chilly night."

Meekly Milly gathered small dead branches, built a cone, lit it at the bottom, and the dancing flame spread up, lit the section of road where they stood. The clatter of Rathbone's riders died. The only sounds then were the faint downdraft blowing off the higher hills, sighing through the wall of trees, and the firecracker-snapping of the twigs.

But even these insignificant noises were sufficient to cover Sam Allee's soft footfalls on the dusty road as he moved up behind Petrie. The first the big man knew of another presence was the crashing blow of Sam's rifle butt against the back of his head. Sam chose that way rather than a shot that could bring Rathbone back, but he misjudged the hardness of Petrie's thick skull. The man collapsed and Allee assumed he was out, his prime concern swinging to the girl. He stepped toward her.

He did not see Petrie's hand grab at his ankle. He was jerked off his feet and fell on his side, the rifle in his left hand under him. His breath was knocked out, stunning him for the moment, and Petrie took advantage. The brawny outlaw might have drawn his gun and shot, might have used the knife that hung in a sheath at the back of his thick neck. He did neither. Proud of his bull strength, his capability at barroom fighting that had killed more than one man with only his fists, he rolled astride of Sam Allee and clamped his fingers tight around the throat.

Sam let go of the rifle to use both hands against the stranglehold. He fought to get a grip on one thick finger, to bend it back and break it, but Petrie was much too strong. Allee could not pry up even the smallest talon enough to get his own around it. His air cut off, unable to breathe, his vision blurred to a crimson fog, his ears roared in a growing thunder. He was losing consciousness but hazily trying to will a warning to the girl to escape while Petrie was occupied with choking him.

The shot sounded dull and far away. Instantly the vise around Allee's throat relaxed, and Petrie's heavy weight collapsed on his chest and head. Allee sucked air in noisy gasps, not understanding anything more than that he was alive and the fight was over. He lay inert, unable to move, pinned to the ground, as consciousness returned and the red haze cleared. He felt the body on top of him move, and thought the man was attacking again, and heaved himself over to throw the weight off. It rolled away. He opened his eyes. Milly Wertz was bent above him, a heavy, smoking gun in one hand, tugging with the other at Petrie's belt. Blood from a gaping wound just under Petrie's ear spilled down the brute neck through a dark sear of powder burn. Allee kicked free, sat up, and saw that the outlaw's holster was empty, comprehended then that the redhead had drawn Petrie's own gun, put the muzzle against his neck, and killed him with the single shot.

She shoved the gun at Allee, dug hers from Petrie's pocket, holstered it, saying urgently, "Get up, Sam. Hurry. The shot will bring the others back any minute." With her hands free she took Allee's arm, pulling him as he tried to rise, supporting and guiding him as he staggered to Petrie's horse. "Can you mount? Can you stay in the saddle?"

His legs were shaking but he made it up, hauling himself by the horn. The ringing in his ears was fading, but his lungs burned. He needed time to recover strength. They did not have it. He sat slack, hanging to the horn to keep from falling off.

"Go on. Get clear." The words were a croak.

Instead the girl swung up on Ginger, snatched Petrie's reins, yanked on them, pulling the big horse after hers. The eastern sky was lightening when she took the animals at a fast walk back to where Sam had broken through the timber, gathered in the livery horse, drove it across the creek, and forded after it. By the time they climbed the far bank, Sam Allee had steadied and could ride alone. Milly gave him his reins, and, towing the livery animal, cut through the timber, uphill, angling toward the canyon and the ford in front of the store. She did not try to conceal their tracks. Haste was the most important matter, to reach the family community before they were overtaken.

They ran the animals even though the footing was rough, reached the shallow bar and splashed across the creek, lurched up to the high ground of the yard and crossed that, the girl yelling an alarm.

As they drove to her cabin her brother jumped through the door, belting his trousers around his waist, his gun-belt slung over his arm, shouting his question. "What's after you?" He saw Sam Allee and bawled, "What's he doing here?"

She panted at him. "Get the ram's horn. Wake the clan. Sam's outlaw crew double-crossed him and they're chasing us. They want to kill him and steal his herd and ranch. Go quickly."

"Ain't nobody here. There was a stomp last night up at Tom's, and they stayed over." Rob Wertz jumped off the porch barefoot, running, slapping his belt around him, heading for the store.

Milly wheeled after him with Sam just behind, calling, "Go for them. We can hold the ford from here until they come."

Rob ran through the door and was back immediately carrying the twisted ram's horn, pausing to send the long, mournful blast through the still morning air, repeated three times, the signal for emergency to anyone within hearing distance. But it could not carry around the mountain foot and up the tortuous canyon. He ran for the trail as Allee and the girl flung down and through the door Rob had left open. Inside the cluttered building Milly ran for rifles, tossed one to Sam, tossed a box of shells, and pointed at one of the two front windows.

"We can stand them off long enough. There's quicksand below the ford and no crossing above it."

Rob Wertz had little more than disappeared among the trees beyond the yard when Rathbone's crowd broke into sight, moving shadows in the dim dawn beginning to creep down the mountain. Sam Allee shoved the lower sash up and heard Milly's window squeal open. He watched the lead rider spur up and down the stretch of shore, looking for tracks in the soft ground, saw him discover them and shove his mount half-way across. Sam fired, heard Milly's gun at the same time and did not know which bullet knocked the rider out of the saddle. The animal, frightened, lunged on through the shallow water, throwing spray, veered away from the buildings, and crashed into the brush.

The rest of the crew had hauled up on the bank to see if the ford was genuine or if the tracks were a trick to tempt them into trouble. As the one in the lead fell, screamed, and was carried downstream in tumbling swirls, they pulled around, driving back into the timber. Their going was noisy even over the roar of the water. Then all sound stopped.

Sam Allee said, "Before they show again, does the store carry guns, one I can buy? This antique of Otto's leaves a little to be desired."

Milly brought him a short gun from a case under a counter. With that loaded and shoved in his holster he felt more ready for whatever lay ahead. With the girl returned to her window and he at his they waited, watchful, for the men to reappear across Pinkham Creek.

12

Sounding far away, the ram's horn blew again within the mouth of the canyon. Dawn crept down the opposite mountainside, touching the tips of the lower trees. There was no movement across the creek for a long spell, then shapes appeared detaching themselves from the timber, beyond the range of the rifles in the store, and rode to the bank with the clear intention of crossing below the ford.

None of Butch Rathbone's outlaws knew Pinkham Creek, its obvious and hidden treacheries. Sam Allee watched them with no twinge of compassion, his boyhood memories telling him the discovery they would soon make. Again they sent a lone scout into the water that was still shallow at that point. The horse took a few mincing steps, then began to sink, flounder, drawn chest-deep into the unstable sand bottom. The rider saw the danger, kicked out of the stirrups, yelling for a rope. A noose was thrown, dropping over one upward extended arm, was jerked tight, and the man was dragged from his saddle just as the thrashing horse went under.

Milly Wertz's laugh was cold as the rider was towed ashore, her voice acid. "They'll think twice before they try that again. Keep an eye out now for them to go up beyond the ford and find they can't cross there either." She stood her rifle beside the window, adding, "I don't know about you but I'm plain starved. I'll fix us something before the boys come down."

The long night had been so full of tension that Sam Allee had not thought of food, but mention of it brought quick ravenous hunger. There was a flat-topped iron heating stove at the back of the store, and the girl built up a fire, brought the half-full coffee pot forward over the open hole, and sliced side meat from the slab hanging from a rafter onto the black grill.

Allee kept the vigil as the light grew. The crew went back to the timber, reappearing later where he expected them. Grouped on the bank near the far bend, they apparently argued the possibility of the horses swimming the fast current. One was delegated, tied a rope around his middle, and jumped his animal almost to the center of the sluicing water. The horse landed belly-deep but was immediately swept off its feet. The rope jerked the rider out of the saddle and while he was pulled back, tumbled beneath the surface most of the time, the horse was rolled over and over, carried down to the ford where it fought to stand. Then it bolted for the yard and stood trembling in terror.

Allee took a grim pleasure in Butch Rathbone's increasing frustration. From the stove the cooking smells, meat, frying potatoes, pan biscuit, coffee, drifted toward the open window in such tantalizing strength that his own frustration at the time the cooking took was physically painful. When Milly brought a plate piled high and a steaming cup, balancing them on the windowsill, he wolfed it all, wincing as he finally poured the coffee down. In his mind no coffee in the world could stand against the lye brewed on the stoves of Kings Canyon. He had his pet theory about why these mountain people lived so long, that the alcohol, caffine, nicotine they consumed were a poisonous shield against the most virulent of invading bugs.

Up by the bend the crew again withdrew out of sight, and Allee could picture the angry conference. For awhile he thought he could hear them shouting, then he saw the Wertz clan burst in a ragged line out of the canyon, loping for the store, and for the moment the danger of a concerted rush across the ford was over. Doc Wertz's brother Tom was at the head of the pack, clinging astride his son Pete's back, shaking one fist over his head. Pete stomped into the store, eased the old man down to a chair, and the rest trooped in after him. At the rage flaming in Tom's face Milly Wertz shoved Sam Allee against the wall beside the window and blocked him there with her body.

Tom was already shouting. "I told you to stay away from here and I meant it. This time by damn I'll shoot you myself."

It was not an idle threat. There was less than no help here unless Sam could get past the blind fury, make the patriarch comprehend what was happening in the Park before a Wertz bullet put an end to his whole fight.

To catch the man's attention he shouted, emptied his lungs. "Shut up."

It stopped the tirade. Into the shocked silence Allee reached for breath to go on but Milly beat him to the words, and she was not redheaded for nothing.

Fists on her hips, she pushed her face toward Tom. "You old fool, where's your brains? If that hardcase lot has its way they'll be camped square on our doorstep, and they won't stop there. We either get rid of them now or our lives aren't worth a wood nickel."

Tom reared back, blinking at this rare challenge to his authority, then growled at her. "It's the Allees' fight, not ours. Let them . . ."

"Let them nothing. You're going to sit still and let Rathbone take over the canyon? Since when did the Wertz family let anybody run us off our land? I'm ashamed of you."

Old Tom growled again, this time more like a

wolf than a man, and in a changed tone asked, "Well, if it's like that, where are they now?"

"In the timber over across. Sam and I stood them off, then the quicksand and the sluice stopped them. You can rush the ford now before they know you're doing it."

The old man moved his head from side to side slowly. With his decision taken he was thinking again, using the cunning of long experience. He knew his country intimately, every cut, every brush thicket, rock burst, stream, and tree.

"You've said your piece, missy, but I'll run this show. Rob, you and Hans take some boys down this side of Pinkham through the timber to the Laramie road and stake out there. Pete and the rest of us will go over and drive them back against your line. Your job is to see they don't get away as we run them down to you. We'll give you fifteen minutes start before we move."

"That's better." There was pride now in the girl's voice. "That sounds like the way Doc would do if he was here."

It was a peacemaking gesture, and the old man accepted it with a surprising wink for his little spitfire niece. Then the crowded room turned busy. Most of the men emptied out through the rear door after Rob, heading for the community barn and their horses. They were replaced by those filling the yard for whom there had not been space inside, and Tom repeated the orders for them.

That contingent went out to saddle and came back to wait. Milly carried the black two-gallon coffee pot that always simmered on the stove to the rear counter. A whiskey barrel sat there above a shelf filled with battered tin cups that were seldom washed. She half-filled the cups with coffee, and the men drew them to the brim from the barrel.

Sam Allee had grown up on the mixture here and helped himself as he had in boyhood, hoping that once again he would be accepted as a friend if they credited him with helping to save the canyon from Rathbone. He was keyed up to a high tension, looking ahead to the fight, knowing that his hardcase crew would not be defeated without some losses among the mountain people that he might be blamed for and relying on the whiskey to quiet him down some.

When fifteen minutes had gone by, the men left the cups on the counter and took their rifles out to the horses. Sam Allee caught up the livery animal he had ridden from Cowdry, mounted, and joined the others at the barn. Old Tom Wertz was being hoisted into a saddle and handed a rifle, though Sam wondered if the shriveled figure could even stay aboard.

The family leader discovered him and straightened fiercely. "You ain't riding, Allee."

"The hell I'm not."

There was a long moment of challenge between them, then Wertz shrugged. "Come on then, but stay in back of me and follow orders."

In the lead he walked his animal around to the front yard with Sam and some forty tribesmen following, then sunk his spurs and charged the ford. The splash of their crossing sounded like lashing rain. They were halfway through the icy creek when a gun flashed from the edge of timber. A horse behind Sam screamed and went down. Over his shoulder Sam saw the rider thrown, saw the animal's thrashing hoof crash against the man's head, split it open, saw the body tumbled downstream.

Tom Wertz saw too and yelled the name of his older son, Pete. He lost his head. Without his brother Doc there to control him, Tom went berserk. He jammed his spurs deep again, jumped his horse up the far bank, drove straight for the spot from which the shot had come. Behind Sam the cousins tried to shout the warning, tried to stop him. Sam spurred to head him off, turn him away. He was still one jump behind when Tom crashed through the fringe of brush, swinging up his gun too late. Before he could fire, an outlaw kneeling at the base of a tree with his rifle ready, squeezed the trigger. The gun exploded squarely in Tom's gaunt, contorted face. The old man's arms jerked wide, his mount shied from the flash, and the rider pitched off it, already dead.

Sam Allee shot the outlaw. The shouting behind him was joined by more ahead, Rathbone's crew deeper in the timber cursing and thrashing through it. They had dismounted to rest their horses and were scattered among the trees. Now there was a rush to get back to the animals.

Unaware of assuming command Allee swung an arm and rode in hurried pursuit at the head of the mountain tribe, fanning them to a spreading line. He heard the rattle of fire as one and then another of the men he had brought to the Park was spotted and brought down, saw flashes as others stood their ground to fight back, and knew some of the Wertz clan fell. That did not stop the many others. They bore down on the running crew who reached the mounts, flung up, and in sudden panic beat a retreat from the overwhelming attack. There were just too many mountain men for even Butch Rathbone to take on.

The Wertz men paused, gathering around Tom's body and the wounded cousins, milling, not heeding Sam Allee's urging them to follow.

Then he heard another horse splash through the water and Milly's high cry. "Go on. Go after them. I'll look to the boys here."

That from one of their own caught their attention. Yelling, they drove downhill, outdistancing Sam on the tired livery animal. He listened to the chase, waiting for the Rathbone people to ride into the ambush on the Laramie road.

The first muffled shots came. His defected crew curved off along the road but found no escape. As

Sam came out of the timber, dust rose in a pall from the roadway, hiding much of the battle. Gunfire, yells, curses, screaming animals made a tumult for a brief time. Then there was quiet. Through the settling dust Sam saw that the two Wertz parties had what was left of Butch Rathbone's hardcases trapped and surrounded. A bare half-dozen survivors, unless some had managed to get away during the flight down the mountain. Coming up with them, Allee saw the huddled group had been disarmed but stood snarling in defiance, while the Wertz men who had crossed the ford shouted their report of the losses there.

Hans Wertz listened in stunned silence, then raged in a high yell. "They killed Paw and Pete? They'll hang for that, right now."

"No."

They deserved hanging, Sam Allee admitted, but it went against the grain to see the group so helpless here, so vastly outnumbered, the victims of mob vengeance. Yet he was a victim of sorts himself. He read it in the stone faces that turned toward him at his word. For a single moment at the ford when they had lost their leader the Wertz men had followed him, deployed themselves at his order. Their old suspicion of him was now returning. From babyhood they had been taught to hate the name Allee and though because of Doc's friendship with Sam they had tolerated him, even been friendly, Tom's more recent distrust and dislike of him was the opinion that prevailed here. He too was helpless to prevent the hanging. The circle of riders shut him away from the men at the center.

Hans Wertz glared at him, said tonelessly, "Which one's Rathbone?"

"None of them." Sam raised his voice to reach the crew. "Where's Butch?"

They looked toward him, sullen, and kept silent. He could not tell from their expressions whether they knew if Rathbone was alive or dead. In the heavy timber he could be crouching within feet of the road. The thought made Sam's neck hairs crawl. Only the fact that he would betray himself would keep the man from shooting Sam in the back. And until Sam knew that Rathbone was dead he could not ride easy. The Flying A brand was registered to the foreman. Sam would have to be killed to make good the steal, and though this crew was finished the West was filled with the type who would join Rathbone's play.

There was nothing he could do here. He turned the horse away, Hans watching after him for some minutes, suspicious of a try to break the prisoners free.

His stubbornness would not let him quit now. He would head for Walden, enter a formal protest with the county clerk. Sam had the bill of sale for the cattle bought in Nebraska, and with a good lawyer he could make a fight for the herd.

He rode with care, watchful, listening, checking his back trail, half expecting Rathbone or some of his riders who had not been caught to challenge him, but he had seen no one, heard nothing by the time he stopped at the lunchroom at Cowdry, and there was no horse at the rail.

Inside, Emma Devers rested spraddle-legged on a chair behind the counter, a steaming coffee cup before her. She poured one for Allee without being asked, saying immediately, "Lots of men in a hell of a hurry chased by here right after you and Milly lit. What became of them?"

He told her tiredly, "They ran into Milly's clan. Have any strangers come back through here within the past hour?"

Her eyes bird-bright, she nodded. "Big ugly fellow on a used-up horse. Stopped for pie and coffee and didn't pay for either. You took my rifle and I couldn't stop him."

Sam rang a dollar on the counter. "I'll bring the gun by later. Which way did he go?"

"Walden way. Who is he?"

"Thanks. I'll tell you about it next time."

He escaped the questions, went out to the tired horse and did not push it, riding through the open grassland with less worry about being bushwhacked. It was well after noon when he turned in at Otto Schultz's livery. Fritz looked at the condition of the animal, looked at Sam's drawn face, and said nothing about either, but his voice was choked with curiosity as he answered Sam's question. Yes, a big man had come in from the Cowdry road an hour earlier, left a horse that was too tired to eat. Fritz pointed at a box stall where a sweated gelding stood head down, asleep. There could be no doubt. It was Rathbone's horse.

Sam said tonelessly, "Anybody with him?"

"Nope."

"Any other strangers been through today?"

The boy had seen none. Allee stood considering. It could be that Rathbone alone had escaped, or that others had chosen to ride out altogether. Either way it was the big man himself Sam would have to find and settle with before he could consider any further move, if indeed there was any move left open to him.

One of the saloons, he thought, would be the place to begin his search. He left Fritz Schultz, walked to the runway entrance, and stopped there to study the street, the bright sunlight, and the dark shadowed places where the foreman could be lurking. People were on the sidewalk, but Rathbone was not one of them. Sam left the shelter and went to the nearest saloon, looked over the batwings, and did not see his man in the sparse company there. He was turning away when a heavy voice called his name in sharp surprise.

Spinning, Sam discovered the big figure before the

second saloon, the louvers just swinging closed where he had pushed through them. Recovering, Rathbone's clawed hand struck like a snake for his holstered gun. Sam Allee was faster. His gun was in his hand before Rathbone touched leather. He shot once, saw where the bullet hit the stained shirt front, saw the big body stand solid for a second of shock, then crumple, twist down, fall to a huddle, and lie motionless in the grit on the splintered sidewalk.

People were still diving for cover when it was over. A hush fell. Sam Allee holstered his gun without hurry, feeling great weariness roll over him. Then he walked doggedly toward the courthouse and Marshal Gunnison's office.

After reporting there, after visiting Ephraim Dole to claim the Flying A brand as his own, he returned to the livery, told Fritz to warn him if anyone from Seven Rivers showed up, then climbed to the haymow, burrowed in, and fell asleep at once.

13

He slept the clock around and more. The sun was set when voices below aroused him, a man's question, then Otto Schultz's gutteral disclaimer that he had seen Sam Allee that day.

Sam fought out of grogginess, crawled to the ladder and looked down, shoving the gun he had drawn back in its place as he heard Milly Wertz say angrily, "Don't you lie to me, Dutchman. There's the horse he was riding, in that stall. He rode in yesterday. Where is he?"

"Here," Sam called. "Otto didn't lie. I've been up here since last evening." He dropped down the rungs, stiff from the heavy sleep, combing hay out of his face and hair with his fingers, winking his thanks to the old hostler for protecting his hiding place.

Schultz shrugged his thick shoulders, no longer curious or concerned, and waddled to his office.

Standing beside her brother, the mountain girl raked Sam with a long, worried look, let out a slow, relieved breath but spoke tightly. "That big horse at the back, Butch Rathbone used it yesterday. He must be in town now."

Sam Allee nodded. "He is. He's dead. We met on the street. He tried to draw on me. There were witnesses enough to clear me. Did your family lose many boys?"

"Tom and Pete." Rob said it without grief as if the old bully and his slow-witted son were small loss. "A few shot up some, but they'll get over that. So this is the end of it?"

Sam's mouth turned down in bitterness. "For you, I suppose so. For me, it depends. With Rathbone's crew gone how do I take a ranch away from Drake?"

"Get another crew." It was Milly, her voice defiant.

Allee lifted and dropped his shoulders. "More hardcases, the only kind who could do the job? And have them turn on me too? I've learned I can't trust them."

Rob Wertz spoke low, thoughtfully. "That crowd, they weren't riding for you for free, and they wouldn't fight for regular wages. What were you paying them with?"

"A stake I've been setting aside for just that purpose. Why?"

Looking at his feet, kicking at the loose hay in the runway, Rob said tentatively, "Our boys in the hills, they like money too. With Tom gone where he can't interfere, maybe I could talk them into teaming up, ask them whether they'd rather have you or Drake in the saddle down here. You got cash I can show them?"

A new glimmer of hope sparked in Sam Allee. With their long conditioning against the Allee family he doubted that even the highest wages would tempt them to follow him, but it was the last possibility he could think of. He said evenly, "I have it. Buried in the root cellar out at the Allen place. Shall we go get it?"

On the ride Milly was quiet, saying nothing, her thoughts betrayed only by a small secret smile that played around her mouth, unnoticed by the men. For his part her brother showed a marked change from his recent reluctant acceptance of Sam. It was as though Rob had reverted to the old friendship when they were boys and Doc was raising them both, as though Rob again looked on Sam as one of the tribe. He went further, planning ahead to extend the Wertz territory. They would, he dreamed aloud, take over the best of Seven Rivers range, build up the Allen headquarters into a home ranch in the little hollow beside Moss Creek, expand along the Michigan, stretch a line of camps clear across to the Encampment. Sam did not interrupt, wanting Rob's enthusiasm to grow strong enough that if his cash did not win over the tribe into a fighting force, the hope of moving down to the rich grasslands would.

They stopped at Cowdry where Emma Devers slammed plates of supper in front of them, disgruntled that no one would talk to her about the mysterious men who had chased Sam Allee, no one would say what the end of that chase had been. By midnight they had followed the Encampment road to the Allen branch-off and reached the low rise above the old homestead.

Light from the windows made Allee haul up short. Rob Wertz made a guess that some of

Rathbone's crew had escaped and gathered here to wait for their leader. Sam did not think so.

"More likely Drake's crew moving back in," he said sourly. "We only ran off half his crew the other day, and I'm not at all sure they kept going out of the country after Kid Diller was killed. They could all have gone back to the ranch. You two wait here until I scout down there."

Neither argued, and he took that as an omen that the pair at least would accept his leadership. They followed only far enough to take themselves off the brow of the hill so that they were not silhouetted against the star-filled night sky. Sam put his horse ahead, drifting down the slope through the shadows cast by the occasional trees, the animal's hooves making no sound on the soft, grass-matted ground.

Approaching the corral, he saw only one horse inside. In his arrogance had his brother again sent a single rider here to maintain his line camp? Sam moved against the fence, whistled softly, and the horse came toward him, nuzzling at the hand he stretched over the top bar. In the pale night light the brand scar on the shoulder showed dimly. Otto Schultz's simple S.

To Sam that ruled out Seven Rivers. Perhaps after all it was a Rathbone man who had lost his mount in the route and made his way afoot to Walden. Sam swung down, tied his horse against the poles, drew his short gun, went quietly to the grimy window, put an eye at the lower corner.

Martha Bollen sat at the table facing him, her head down, dealing a solitaire hand of dirty, well-worn cards.

Seeing her was a shock. She should have left Walden by the morning stage on the day before, heading east. Why she was here and how she had found the location he could not guess. He swung immediately to the door, lifted a hand toward the knob, became aware that he held his gun, and holstered it. Then he knocked, calling at the same time.

"It's me, Martha. Sam Allee."

He pushed the door in and found her standing now, rigid, a little pearl-handled weapon aimed at him. She lowered it as he stepped in, seemed to forget it hanging at her side, looking at him with eyes flared wide as fright slowly went out of them. Sam kicked the door closed with his boot heel.

"Martha. What are you doing here?"

Her mouth did not lift in a smile. Her voice was toneless. "Hiding. Running from Drake and his crew. Yesterday, they stopped the stage from coming into Walden, so I couldn't leave. Marshal Gunnison kept them from taking me out of the hotel overnight, but this morning they kept the stage away again and Achey Collins . . . Drake sent him word to put me out. He did, with the advice to go back to Seven Rivers and behave like a woman should."

Sam Allee's lips thinned to a narrow line. "Who brought you here?"

"That towheaded boy Fritz. I was standing on the street wondering where you might be when he appeared out of nowhere and took me down the alley to the livery. He saw I was frightened and gave me this gun that had been his mothers; then he saddled two horses and slipped me out of town. Then he told me you were sleeping in the haymow but with Seven Rivers in Walden he wasn't going to risk their finding you. He said for me to wait and he'd send you out when you waked up."

Sam Allee groaned. All this had happened while he had been running and fighting Rathbone's crew, while he had lain exhausted in the livery. And he was grateful to young Fritz, but the girl was not safe here, for sooner or later Drake would try to reclaim the place.

Also, glad as he was to see her, she was another complication. He had not intended to spend time here, and meant to dig up the money, ride immediately to Kings Canyon to see if the Wertzes could be recruited. He could not take Martha Bollen there. Some instinct warned him not to throw her and Milly Wertz together again, though he did not pause to think it through. Then the solution came. He could send Milly and Rob ahead with the money, follow with Martha as far as Cowdry, and leave her with Emma Devers to wait for the next stage. Emma would be delighted to be part of an intrigue to frustrate Drake Allee.

They would have to move soon. Now. Get away from this place. Not only for her safety but because he must have a new fighting crew before his trail herd arrived, and that could be any day now. It left little time to win the mountain tribe to his side. He started to explain when a sound outside made him stiffen, then he remembered Milly and Rob and judged they had followed him. He groaned again, seeing no help for them finding the blonde girl here, turned, and pulled the door open.

He stood frozen. Men were outside. One ahead of the others was on foot: The brother he was here to fight.

Drake Allee was as astonished as Sam. Drake had ridden to Walden leisurely, expecting to find Martha Bollen crushed, helpless, cast out on the street. When he did not, it had taken time to locate someone who had seen her ride off at the side of the livery boy. Since his younger brother was the only person in the country she could have had enough contact with to turn to, his guess was that she would head for this line camp.

But he had not believed Sam Allee would be here. Drake had posted riders in the ragged hills around the homestead to watch it after his crew was run off. Their report was of a running fight in which at least some of Sam's hardcases had turned against him, that he had fled for the mountains with the gunmen in pursuit.

Yet here he stood in the open doorway. For moments they stared at each other.

Drake's belated reaction was to slap for his gun as Sam dropped a hand toward his. Both were too late.

Martha Bollen had been quicker, throwing herself between the men, clamping both small hands around Drake's thick wrist before he drew, crying fiercely, "No. No. No, Drake. No, Sam. Stop . . ."

Both men froze again, Drake's hot eyes falling to the girl's face, holding on it. This was the city girl he had brought West to marry. The woman who had defied him. The vixen who had rushed from him to another man for help. Worst of all, the one she had turned to was the half brother he despised.

He tried to shake loose but she clung tight. Savagely he told her, "Get out of the way."

"I won't. Let go of that gun."

There was no relaxing in the man. Across her head he bit at Sam Allee. "You can't even fight your own fight. You hide behind a woman's skirt."

Sam's temper, never even where Drake was concerned, blazed coldly, was icy in his tone. "Martha, get back."

"No." She did not turn to look at him, still hanging to Drake's wrist, shaking it. "I will not stand aside and see you two kill each other. You must both be crazy."

Drake snapped, "I told you before this does not concern you."

"Doesn't it?" Her shrill words hit at him. "It should not concern me that the man I came here to marry is on the verge of murdering his own brother?"

"You refused to marry me."

She shook the wrist harder, forcing him to look away from Sam, down to the wild, pleading blue eyes, to listen to the rush of words.

"That isn't true. I said I wouldn't marry you as long as you meant to run Sam out of the Park or have him killed. You don't have to do either."

The handsome face changed, turned triumphant. Even smiled stiffly. "You will still marry me, Martha?"

"That depends on you, Drake. How you act. How much you want me."

Sam Allee had the unreal sensation of standing at a window looking in on other people's lives. His strong impulse was to leave, to let them quarrel in private. But there was no way of getting out. Drake's big body blocked the door, and beyond him were the mounted men, taking no hand for fear of shooting their boss by accident.

Sam saw it as a standoff for the moment. He expected Drake to whirl, throw the girl aside, and if he could not fire himself, at least leave the way open for his crew to gun Sam down.

Into that moment a gun spoke off in the darkness. Either Milly or Rob Wertz declaring themselves. The bullet struck a horse. It reared, unseating the startled rider. The rest of the riders scattered, wheeling to the shadows as the lone gun blazed again. This time they saw a muzzle flash, and Drake Allee's crew fired toward it from several directions. There was no answering sound to tell if any of the shots had scored. There was no further shooting.

Drake said to no one in particular, "Now who do you suppose that is out there."

Hank Lofter growled from somewhere near, "I don't know, but I'm going to find out fast."

Sam Allee saw a horse move away through the dark. Until he had heard the voice he had not known Drake's foreman was here. It brought a flash of fear for Milly and Rob Wertz, for Lofter had shown himself to be brutal, like Rathbone, a man who would not hesitate to shoot both Wertzes from ambush if he could locate them. He thought of shouting a warning but knew the sound would not carry far enough, through the door and around the corner, up the hill. He could not tell what the continuing silence meant, whether the girl and her brother expected the Seven Rivers crew to be spreading out, moving toward them through the night, and had retreated, or were waiting where he had left them, watching for a target. Or had they moved to where they could see the lighted doorway?

Drake still stood framed there, facing the room, his broad figure plainly silhouetted for anyone who wanted to put a bullet into it. Sam held his breath. He did not want his brother shot in the back, however much hatred there was between them, and prayed that if the Wertzes saw him they would mistake him for Sam, since they were near the same size and shape.

But it was imperative to break this deadlock. He had to get through the door Drake blocked so effectively, to get into the open where he could be heard. He spoke evenly to Martha Bollen. "Hold his gun arm tight."

She did, throwing her body across it, pressing it against her with all her strength. Without warning, Sam swung over her shoulder, drove a fist into Drake's exposed jaw as hard as he could. The head snapped back, the knees buckled, Drake went down, sitting rather than falling, dragging the girl on top of him. Sam knew his brother was not really out; the blow had had to travel too far, but the man was stunned.

Sam did not give him time to recover. He leaped over both bodies, charging out, spinning into the dark. He heard nothing, could not judge where anyone was in the thick shadows. He could barely distinguish the darker line of timber and made for that, running, the thick grass cushion deadening the sound of his footsteps. He shouted once.

"Wertz. Keep down. Don't fire."

That would not tell the crew how many others were around, and if he could make the timber, he could fire toward the building, draw attention off Milly and Rob. But he did not know whether they had changed position. Any moving shadow could be either one of them or a Seven Rivers rider.

He ran lightly, his gun ready in his hand, seeing no one until a horseman loomed suddenly on the rise ahead, bulking dark against the lighter sky. He called again. Wertz. If the rider were Milly or Rob they would recognize his voice and answer.

Instead he drew a shot. In the bad light it missed him. He fired at the flash, heard a grunt, then another, as the rider was knocked off the horse and lit hard. The animal plunged away, swallowed in the dark.

A voice from Sam's right called urgently. "Phil. Phil. You get him?"

There was no answer. Sam judged the rider was dead. He crouched where he was, his body stone-still, but he seethed with impatience to be running again.

Ahead at the edge of timber a rifle exploded, the bullet whining high over his head. At once a volley broke out and he knew with sickening certainty that the flash they were firing at had pinpointed either Milly or her brother.

14

Sam Allee's head swiveled, seeing muzzles wink in a half circle. Seven Rivers had apparently spread to a curved line, were working forward, crowding toward the dark trees. He was behind them. They were between him and the gun in the timber. It fired from a different spot and another volley tracked it.

Sam began shooting, far to the side, not expecting to hit anything, only to draw fire away from the single gun. The diversion did not fully work. Three shots reached for him, but Seven Rivers pushed on, loud now, shouting back and forth among themselves to identify their locations, Hank Lofter's voice clubbing louder than the rest with orders to rout the gunman out.

The Wertz pair would hear the charge and surely they would drift back quietly, then spur for safety. Sam ran forward at full stride, driven by desperation. If they had not come here to help him, neither Wertz would now be in danger.

The tone of the shouts now in the timber changed to triumph. Plainly the crew had found Milly or Rob or both. Sam's lungs ached from his hard running; his head spun from lack of air. He reached for breath and used it all in a high cry.

"Lofter. Hank Lofter. Sam Allee here. Hurt either of those kids and I'll kill you."

He had a harsh laugh for answer as he dived into the shelter of the trees. Twenty feet ahead a match flickered, a lantern was lit. The glow spread over a circle of six riders, their heads turned in his direction. His legs pumped on. He ran unmindful that a few more strides would take him into the light, make him a clear target for their guns.

But no shot came. It was as if they could not believe he would run headlong against them, as if uncertainty stayed their hands. Then the circle split as if to let him rush into a trap, a trap he ignored, for as the horses separated he saw what had been hidden in the center.

Milly Wertz lay crumpled on the ground. She looked like a small, abandoned rag doll, unmoving, lifeless. Her calico dress bore a dark stain above her breast where a bullet had slammed in just below her shoulder.

A cry of hurt, of rage, of futility wrenched from Sam Allee. His rifle dropped from his hand as he flung himself on the loamy earth at her side. Rob Wertz was already kneeling on her other side, his narrow, bony face streaked with tears that furrowed through the dust coating his cheeks, one trembling hand pressing his neckerchief against the flowing wound. Around them the circle of men dismounted slowly, stood silent and uneasy. They were a hard crew when fighting against men, but aside from Lofter they respected women, would not knowingly gun down one, and the pathetic huddle shamed them.

Ignoring them all Sam choked out one word. "Dead?"

Rob shook his head, babbling. "I've got to stop the bleeding. I've got to stop the bleeding." He sounded in shock, as though his mind did not fully comprehend that his sister had been shot, as though he had forgotten the encircling enemy, as completely as had Sam.

Allee took the soaked handkerchief from Rob and with a stiff forefinger forced a wadding into the small, blue-rimmed hole. Despite all of the pain he knew that would cause Milly Wertz did not react with so much as a quiver.

He straightened then to his knees, his eyes dangerous on Hank lofter. "Who did this?"

The foreman's tone rasped without regret. "How the hell do I know? In the dark we couldn't tell who was shooting at us. We shot back. A girl plays with firearms, what does she expect?"

All control snapped inside Sam Allee's head. Unaware of what he did, he charged up in a lunge across the girl that brushed past Rob, his hands outstretched, clawed. Unconscious of exhaustion from the run, of legs near-paralyzed, his anger was so fierce it drove all feeling from his body. Like a spring released he caught Lofter wholly unprepared; his head butted into the broad, thick chest, drove the man back to trip and fall over one of his own men.

Sam's weight crushed down on both of them. For a moment none of them could move. The breath was knocked out of the rider on the bottom. He lay gasping. Lofter grunted, gasped, recovered enough to try to roll from under Sam Allee, but Sam's reaction was too fast. Both claws clamped around the big foreman's neck and tightened, instinct squeezing out life.

Lofter was strong but Sam's fury doubled his strength. The man he throttled fought back, pounded a right, then a left into Sam's ribs. In his blind concentration Allee felt neither blow. His fingers constricted further, crushing.

Hank Lofter fought for air, desperate now, his face red, blotching toward purple. Two men jumped in, grabbed Allee's shoulders, tried to haul him off their strangling foreman. Sam dug one boot toe deep, kicked back with the other, a piston stroke to a stomach that sent the man arcing, lifted him over the lantern, sprawled him on his shoulders. The second man jumped on Sam's back, locked an arm rigid around Sam's neck, grabbed Sam's thick hair with the other hand, and yanked back, all but snapping Sam's spine.

Despite the pain, the pressure, Sam's fingers remained locked. The man on his back let go of Sam's windpipe, used both hands to pry up the center finger of Sam's left hand, to bend it back savagely until the bone snapped.

Excruciating pain like striking lightning lanced through Sam Allee's arm, filled his entire body, jarred him out of the insane rage. He could no longer maintain the intense pressure on Lofter's throat. His grip relaxed and in that moment the man astride him yanked him off the foreman, rolled him to his back on the unyielding ground. At once the others were on him in a pack, spreadeagling him, pinning him. One jumped hard on his unprotected stomach, would have convulsed him had Sam not been held. Air pumped out of him.

A voice yelled. "Stop. Look. Over here."

Hank Lofter was sitting, head down, holding his throat. Beside him Rob Wertz had his rifle jammed against the thick neck, his finger tense on the trigger.

"Get away from him. Get back or I fire."

The men stiffened, took one backward step, but the one who had jumped on Sam laughed harshly. "Drop that thing before you get hurt too."

Rob lifted the gun only long enough to shoot the rider, knocking him over dead, then the muzzle was against Lofter again. It was enough. The crew quit, stood frozen, sure now that any move would trigger Lofter's death, as the foreman sat dazed, sucking air. Rob stood away from him, where a sudden twist and grab could not snag his leg, leaned forward, and prodded the muzzle hard against the neck until Lofter realized the situation and slowly lifted both hands shoulder high.

The mountain boy told them through clenched teeth, "Killers. Put your hands on your heads. I'll get every one of you if Milly dies." Without looking away from them he added, "Sam, can you sit up yet?"

Allee could not speak, but he rolled to his knees.

Rob continued. "Stay down like that. Take Lofter's guns, then the rest of them."

Crawling, his focus still blurred, Sam Allee pulled Lofter's short gun, threw it into the dark, found the rifle the foreman had dropped, and flung it away. Then one after the other he gathered the other arms and threw them where they could not be reached without a major rush by the riders. When they were disarmed, he went on all fours to the quiet girl, saw the rise and fall of her breast, and went on to her brother.

"She's breathing," he croaked. "The bleeding's stopped. I'll watch these. You run their horses off but keep two, take them down. There's a spring wagon behind the shed, harness inside. Hail the cabin before you go in. Tell Drake Milly's badly hurt, shot. He'll honor help for a woman. Hitch up and come back so we can take her to Walden."

While he talked he got to his feet, braced them apart, moved close to Rob, and took the rifle from him, careful that the trigger was not pulled as it changed hands. He did not watch after the boy, kept his attention on the crew as he ordered them to lie on their faces in a line in front of Lofter, their arms outstretched beyond their heads. He heard the pound of hooves as the mounts were scattered, the soft swish through the grass as Rob rode one and led another out of the trees, into the deep grass. Shortly he heard Rob's high shout.

"Hello, the house. Drake Allee, this is Rob Wertz. Your crew shot my sister bad. I'm coming for the spring wagon. I'm not armed."

There was silence, then a faint answer. "Come in where I can see you. If you're trying a trick I can shoot you before you find me."

Sam waited, tense, trusting that Drake would not

lower himself before the girl he apparently still wanted, would not murder the boy.

Rob Wertz was not so trusting. Ahead waited the man who was his lifelong enemy, the only man in the country he truly feared. In ordinary circumstances he would give Drake Allee the widest berth possible. Now he had no choice but to ride toward him.

He walked the animals across the meadow, his face sweated, rode a straight line toward the shaft of light from the open cabin door, hauling up nervously just at the edge of it. Drake Allee's voice came raw from the shadows against the wall.

"Come on. Come on. Let's have a look at you."

Holding a deep breath Rob toed the animal he rode, stepped it into the glow and stopped again, both hands lifted away from his sides. He sensed rather than saw movement as Drake circled him out of sight, not showing himself until he was certain there was no rifle in the boot, no gun in the boy's holster, then walked into view ten feet away.

"All right, Wertz, get down."

Rob slipped from the saddle cautiously, turned to face the man.

Drake Allee said, "What was all the shooting?"

"Please," Rob hated to use the word. "Let me get the wagon. Milly could die any minute. If she doesn't reach the doctor . . ."

Drake cut him short. "Where's my damn brother?"

"Back there. But . . ."

"They caught him?"

"We caught them. The crew. We need . . ."

Drake cursed. "I'll soon change that."

He strode toward the horse Rob led, yanked the line out of his hand, set a foot in the stirrup. Rob screamed at him. Then Martha Bollen was through the door, once again catching Drake's arm, shaking it, her voice riding up.

"If you expect ever to marry me, stop this."

Allee looked around, said savagely, "I'll marry you or have you without marriage. Take your choice."

"You could never hold me that way. Drake, I'll marry you, but only if you give up this senseless quarrel. This country is surely wide enough, big enough for both of you and many more."

The man dropped his foot to the ground, dropped the reins, faced her squarely. Strong-willed, he admired strong will in others, had recognized this girl's strength in St. Louis and known she would make the only kind of wife who would satisfy him. He had never met her equal.

As Drake's mind ran swiftly over the conditions, Rob Wertz bent for the drooping reins, raced both horses behind the shed, left them at the wagon, and ran for the harness. He had it tossed on the wagon tongue, was throwing the saddles off the animals by feel when both Drake Allee and the blonde girl came running with a lantern, Drake catching up the harness.

"Here, let me give you a hand."

Rob swung, stood stupid in surprise.

Martha Bollen spoke quickly. "Hurry, boy. If he helps and saves your sister I'll marry him. If she dies I am going to marry Sam."

Rob was too amazed to answer. He dragged the second saddle off as Drake expertly fitted and tightened the harness, snapping orders at the boy as though he belonged to the Seven Rivers crew.

"I'll finish here. You hit the corral, fetch the three horses from it, then catch up with us."

Martha Bollen was already on the wagon seat when Rob ran toward the corral. By the time he had caught up the animals that she, Drake, and Sam Allee had ridden here, the wagon was on its way, pulled at a run, jouncing over the uneven ground toward the faint light of the lantern in the timber.

Rob spurred after it, hauled up sharply halfway there when he remembered that a lamp still burned in the cabin, almost turned back, then spurred ahead again. Milly was more important.

The wagon was parked at the edge of the trees when Rob came up, Sam standing in the bed accepting the limp form from Drake's extended arms, lowering it to a mattress of fresh-cut boughs.

Rob dropped off the saddle, running, calling. "Is she alive?"

Sam nodded. "Still unconscious, but she's breathing."

He swung over to the driver's seat at the same time Martha Bollen climbed to the back, settled beside the mountain girl and impulsively laid a hand on the chilly forehead.

Drake was already gone, jogging back to where his crew stood in a dour cluster, slamming words at them. "Follow us in and don't start anything. I'll explain later."

Lofter tried to speak but his throat was too bruised. Another growled. "On what? They spooked off the horses."

Drake made a fast count. "Whistle them in, they didn't spook far. Lofter and I'll ride the wagon."

Another also rode the wagon, the rider Rob Wertz had shot. It made for a crowd but as close as they were packed together no one spoke on the race-fast drive.

Rob Wertz did not ride with them. He sat the horse watching after them, thinking furiously. He was desperately worried about his sister, but Sam Allee was with her. Sam could do anything for her that he himself could. If. If Drake didn't have him killed as soon as the fancy eastern woman turned her back. He did not trust Drake, did not trust any man associated with Seven Rivers ranch.

He not only mistrusted them, they filled him with a bitter hatred. These people had murdered his father, Doc Wertz. Maybe the man who had pulled the trigger was already dead. He thought so, for the Wertz tribe all believed it had been Kid Diller, but the fact remained that if Hank Lofter had not protected Diller, if Drake had not kept him on the crew, Diller would have been gone from the Park before Doc was shot. In Rob's mind they were all equally guilty.

And now Sam Allee was in the middle of them, voluntarily, because of Milly. That told Rob all he needed to know about how Sam felt toward her. He knew too from the way she had been acting since Sam had come home that this was the man she had set her heart on, whether either of them realized it yet or not.

Abruptly Rob sank his spurs and drove hellbent for Kings Canyon and help. Money or no money, it was time the clan moved against the highhanded ranch crowd.

Both Rob and the horse were winded when they reached the store, but the boy found breath enough for the ramshorn to summon whoever was in the surrounding cabins. Eight men answered the call, running, half-dressed, rifles swinging.

Rob stood above them on the porch, panting, pouring out the story in angry bursts. "Lofter ... Drake Allee's crew ... They hit us at the Allen place ... rode us down. They shot Milly. She may be dead."

To save argument he did not tell them it had been his sister who fired first from the hillside, who had kept firing as she ran from place to place, that she had been hit only a second after her gun had exploded for the last time. There was no time to waste.

He added only, "And they've got Sam Allee. We were out there for his money that he was going to give us to fight for him. Lots of it. They all went to Walden. Let's ride."

The upturned narrow faces tightened with every

word. The long-pent-up anger was ripe for bursting. As he finished they broke apart, toward the cabins for the rest of their clothes and guns, then to the barn for horses. Rob headed that way first for a fresh animal, satisfied with himself. He had asserted himself. The cousins had listened with the respect they had given old Doc. He was beginning to play the role he should inherit, to become the accepted leader of the clan.

Nine hard-faced mountain men, plus two who had joined them not knowing why they were riding, were there out of family loyalty; they pushed through the night. On reaching Walden they pounded to the head of the main street, drew up to a walk, and eased toward the closest saloon. The light from its doorway fell across the group of Seven Rivers horses at the rail there. Just short of those they stopped, stepped quietly from the saddles, tied their animals.

Again Rob asserted himself, issuing orders. "Six of you go through the alley to the back door. We'll wait in front. When we see the door open we'll jump from here, whipsaw them."

With a cocked finger he designated who should take the back; the rest he beckoned behind him and walked cat-footed to the side of the louvers, stopping where he could see, at an angle, the backbar mirror and its reflection of the long room.

The view was a disappointment. There were the bartender and the Seven Rivers crew at the counter. No one else. He had expected to see Drake Allee but the rancher was not there. Either Drake had taken Martha Bollen to the hotel or they were all at the doctor's office. Wherever he was, it was Drake Rob Wertz wanted most.

The rear door opened slightly. A man with a leveled shotgun eased through, then two with revolvers, entering unnoticed, lining along the back wall. At the front Rob slipped through the swinging panels, stepping to one side. The spring hinges squealed. One man at the bar stiffened, turned his head.

The Wertz with the Greening called sharply. "Hold still. All of you get your hands in the air."

The crew was caught flatfooted. Their heads swiveled to both doors, their expressions owlish, muddled. They and Hank Lofter had been dropped off here as the spring wagon passed on its way to the doctor. They had been drinking steadily, drowning their frustration at Drake's order not to take Sam Allee, bewildered by the reversal. Unsteady on their feet they slowly raised their arms.

All except Lofter at the rear end of the bar.

Lofter had refused when Drake wanted the doctor to examine his sore neck and bed him down. Lofter was proud. It galled him that he had not beaten Sam Allee to a pulp in their fight. Going to the doctor would be admitting that he had lost.

For the same reason, not admitting he was losing here, he refused to lift his arms in surrender. More than a little drunk but not showing it, he turned, squarely faced the men at the rear, deliberately drained his glass, deliberately hurled it at the man with the scatter gun.

The man ducked. The gun bucked. The tight pattern of buckshot took Hank Lofter in the chest, tore it apart. Lofter jarred back, then crumpled.

The crew stared down stupidly at the body. The bartender dropped behind the counter, could be reaching for the shotgun on the shelf there.

Rob Wertz's voice slammed down the room. "Don't try."

There was no further move except the other Wertz men drifting through the doors.

15

The miles between the Allen homestead and Walden stretched an interminable distance for Sam Allee. He ached to maintain the first driving speed but the horses were mismatched, were not used to harness, and would not hold a course at the high run. He slowed them to a steadier gait, calling again and again over his shoulder to ask Martha Bollen if Milly Wertz had regained consciousness.

She had not by the time they reached the town. Drake rode the seat beside his brother with Lofter on his other side, both rigid, their eyes straight ahead, not speaking until they neared Walden when Drake suggested Lofter see the doctor. Without answering Lofter had then dropped off the wagon.

Sam broke his silence. "Is Perkins still where he used to be?"

He got a curt nod from Drake, turned the next corner, and reined in before the frame building opposite the courthouse where the physician kept living quarters in the rear rooms and his office at the front.

"Get him up."

Drake Allee dropped off the seat, stalked to the door, and pounded until a querulous voice inside demanded sleepily who was there.

"Allee. Open up, Perkins. We've got a girl here who's been shot."

There was a muffled curse, a light was made, bolts rattled, then the front door was pulled wide.

Drake said sourly, "What have you got so valuable you lock up this tight?"

The doctor was tall, nearly bald, the skull narrow and the eyes sunken behind a beak nose. He looked anything but inspiring in a shank-length nightshirt and crocheted cap.

"Laudanum." The tone matched Drake's. "People get the habit, they'll steal what they can't buy. Where's the girl?"

Drake stood aside. Sam had secured the team, lifted Milly from the bed, and now carried her through the door. The lamp showed her face dead white, her lips colorless. Perkins snorted, waved a hand toward the examination table, and trailed Sam as he laid the still figure on it. Behind them Martha Bollen hurried in, and Drake closed the door after himself.

The room was quiet while Perkins worked, sure-fingered, deft, twisting the red, wet handkerchief out of the hole, cutting a flap out of the stained dress. He bent close, pressing the flesh around the wound, snorting again when Sam asked in a near whisper if she would live, raising a piercing glance at Sam.

"She lose a lot of blood?"

"I wasn't there when it happened, but when I got to her it was all over her, her clothes. Can you save her, Doc?"

Perkins' look was withering. "Bullet's high, didn't pierce the lung, but it has to come out. You got the belly to help?"

Sam flinched. He had seen other wounds probed for bullets and been sickened by the quivering flesh, but he nodded. Perkins turned away to the kerosene stove in the corner, lit it, and moved a tea kettle over the flame, then padded through to the living quarters without a word. He was back shortly, tucking a shirt into butternut pants, still barefoot, stopping in front of Martha Bollen.

"And how strong is your stomach? I need two to hold her down if she wakes before I'm finished."

Sam caught his breath. "She can't do that."

Perkins said irritably, "I don't expect her to. That's yours and Drake's job. I want her to hand me instruments, bandage. Stand over here, ma'am. And don't faint on me."

The eastern girl took her place opposite the doctor. Drake Allee braced his hands on Milly's knees, pressing down. At the head of the table Sam held her arms against the padded table. Looking down at the pale face, the slender figure, he was shocked at how small she seemed. Ordinarily she was so brimming with life and vigor that her size went unnoticed. Now, lying unconscious, unmoving, she appeared shrunk, a child's body except for the swell of breast exposed by the calico flap.

Perkins was humming now, a soft, low sound, as though after all the years surgery was still a fresh and fascinating challenge to enjoy. Sam Allee clenched his teeth against the grating on his nerves. The doctor spread what he would want on the small table beside Martha: a pan of boiling water, a probe dropped into that, forceps, bandage, cotton, jars, and bottles. With alcohol, he washed the blood from the area of the wound then poured liquid over a cotton wad, ether or chloroform by the smell that permeated the room, placed the wad over Milly's nose. She did not stir.

Perkins' lips moved as he counted, timing the anesthetic; then he removed the cotton, dropped it, used the forceps to lift the probe from the steaming water, handing them to Martha.

"Hold it so it doesn't touch anything."

She held the pincers steady. Perkins rammed his hands into the pan, held them there until they were bright red, then shook them partly dry and reached for the probe: he spread the flesh apart and worked the sharp instrument deep.

Under Sam's hands the inert body convulsed once, then was still again. Sweat beaded on Sam's forehead, ran into his eyes as the slender steel searched the hole. He wiped his face against his sleeve, then went back to watching, hynotized, feeling that it was his own chest being operated on.

Minutes passed like hours before Perkins made a sighing sound, partially straightened his bent back and worked the probe upward until a misshapen slug of lead appeared, was brought out, and maneuvered onto the soft mound of solid flesh.

"Ah." The tone was pleased. Perkins prodded at the bullet. "Bone stopped it. Must have been near spent. Now, little lady, if you'll pass me that boric acid and then some bandage, we'll get through here. Anybody have two bucks on them?"

Sam Allee dug in his pocket, almost afraid to ask the question crowding his mind.

"Doc, will she . . . be all right?"

The doctor was insulted. "Why sure, right as rain as healthy as that tribe is, be up and doing in no time. Now, Drake, you know where Emily Pease lives?"

Allee nodded, straightening up off the unconscious girl's knees. "I'll go for her."

"Not so fast, man. Tell her to make up a bed for a patient. We'll move Milly over there."

"Is she a nurse?" Martha Bollen asked.

"Best in four counties. Hell, without her around I'd lose half my cases."

When Drake had gone, Perkins looked Sam over searchingly. "You and your brother patch up your quarrel, did you? What are you looking so peaked about, the girl?"

Sam Allee, now that he was reassured on Milly Wertz's account, was belatedly aware of waves of pain burning through his midsection. He said in embarrassment, "Just a scrap with Lofter. I'll get over it."

The doctor's mouth turned down in disapproval. "Dirty fighter, that one. Peel off your shirt so I can see the damage." When Sam flushed, glancing toward Martha Bollen, Perkins lost his patience. "Come on, come on, if she could do the job she just did, she can stand a look at your belly."

Still coloring, Sam opened the shirt, held the fronts apart, keeping his back to the girl. Perkins studied the mass of red, yellow, purple bruises, took hold of the shirt shoulders, yanked it down off the hands, and tossed it aside.

"Jumped on you with boots. Let's find out how many ribs are broke."

Tenderly he felt over the rib cage, turned Sam about, wrapped his arms around the body, and squeezed lightly, noting the places that drew gasps.

"Three are probably cracked but if they were really busted off you'd yelp a sight more than you did. Missy, pass me that bandage again."

Perkins wrapped yards of cloth around Sam's lower chest, binding it tight, and had just tied the end when Drake returned. A brief, vindictive smile touched Allee's lips at sight of the mottling visible above the wrapping, then he caught Martha's eyes on him and said quietly, "The bed will be ready. How do we carry the girl?"

"Bring the stretcher from the woodhouse while I put on some shoes."

Drake said in an innocent voice, "You go on back to bed, Doc. Sam and I can handle her."

Perkins, already starting for the back rooms, stopped, turned around to face Drake squarely, then to look at Sam and back to Drake. His deep eyes were wise, disturbed, seeing that the trouble between the brothers was not settled after all if the elder Allee wanted to put the younger through the pain of carrying half the stretcher, knowing that Sam would do it out of stubborn pride. He shook his head sadly at these wounds he could not heal.

"I have to see Emily anyway, give her a schedule." The voice was flat, chilly, tossed over his shoulder as he left.

When he returned, the stretcher was on the floor, Drake and Sam lowering Milly Wertz onto it. Perkins tucked a blanket around the girl, managing to shunt Sam away, nodded at Drake, and took up the handles at one end.

"Sam, you fetch my bag, and Missy, you come along."

They made a small parade down the side street to a lighted house with the front door standing open. Emily Pease met them on the porch, showed them inside to a bedroom, and when Perkins positioned the stretcher beside the bed, eased the patient onto it.

A tall, heavy woman, she moved Milly as she would a child, said waspishly, "Poor little thing, hurt this way. I knew her paw, liked him. Them mountain folks hang pretty much to themselves, but my Frank, my husband, he got along with everybody. What you got in mind for me to do for her, Doc?"

She listened to the directions, then beckoned to Martha Bollen. "You stay and give me a hand, dearie. We'll get her clothes off and put a gown on her, be more comfortable when she wakes up. The rest of you, shoo."

Perkins carried the stretcher back to the porch, wondering if there was not something he could do to bring the Allee brothers together, pausing on the top step.

"I could use a drink about now. How about you boys joining me?"

Drake growled at him. "I've got another chore. One of my hands is dead in the buggy. I'll have to take him . . ."

A shotgun blast from the direction of the saloon far up the main street cut him short.

Drake Allee swore harshly. "My crew. They're up there."

The three ran. The oblong of light from the saloon door showed them figures moving in through it. There had been no other shots by the time they arrived, Drake Allee a length ahead of Perkins and Sam, barging into the room. Over Drake's shoulder Sam saw a frozen tableau, the Seven Rivers riders backed against the bar with their hands over their heads, a crowd of mountain men holding guns on the crew. Then he saw the body on the floor.

The noise of their entry brought Rob Wertz spinning toward Drake, stopped in the doorway, nearly hiding the two behind him. Rob's slow smile was cold.

"Just the man we wanted to see. Come in."

Drake stalked forward, seeming not to hear the words, his eyes on Hank Lofter's twisted, bloody body. His voice was hard, dry. "Who did that?"

"I did." The man with the shotgun raised it on Drake's middle. "Put your hands up before you get the same dose."

The elder Allee moved only his head, turning it in disbelief that anyone in the Park would dare threaten him. He said icily, "Getting pretty big for your britches, aren't you?"

The man sneered. "No, *Mister* Allee. The time when we had to kiss the ground for you is gone. Want to know why? I'll tell you. We're going to hang you. Along with your damn crew that shot Milly. You've just gone too far."

Sam, incredulous, stepped past Drake toward Rob Wertz. "Have you all lost your minds?"

The new clan leader's eyes were hot. "Zeke is right and you know it. You ought to thank us. With them dead you'll have your range, all of it."

Sam Allee understood that they were too keyed up to listen, that reason would not reach them. Rob had already swung back to Drake, on whom all the attention centered. Sam moved slowly, knowing a quick action would bring on a mass murder. Drawing his gun quietly he eased closer to Rob Wertz until he stood just behind him, then put the muzzle against Wertz's spine and raised his voice to cover the room.

"I will shoot Rob at the first move. Stand still and think. This is no good."

They stood, their eyes changing from puzzlement to anger at him. He expected that, for in part they had come here as his ally, and now he was denying them.

Rob said savagely, "You taking Drake's side now? Why? You ought to be glad to see Milly's murderers hang."

"She isn't dead." Sam's tone still carried. "The bullet is out and she's all right. But you won't be. Hang Drake Allee and this crew, and this Park will explode. Every rancher in it will come after you. You think you can hole up in the canyon and fight them all off? You can't. They'll throw in together and bring in an army. Rob, you know I'm right."

Their faces did not change. Their minds were frozen. Sam shoved the gun harder, enough to make Rob wince. That they understood. Unpredictable themselves, they believed he would shoot a man he had claimed friendship with. He put it into words to further convince them.

"I'll kill him if I have to, to stop you." He let the words hang for a moment, then spoke to his brother. "Drake, send your men out one at a time; then you clear out."

There was no movement behind him. Sam well knew Drake's fierce pride, knew it was almost beyond bearing that he should back down before these people he despised. The moment drew out; then apparently Drake signaled and a rider edged away from the bar, walked out with his hands still high. Another followed, then the others. Last, Sam heard Drake's boot grind against the floor as he turned, heard his hard steps, then the slam of the batwings as Drake flung them apart and went through. From outside they heard the drum of hooves as the horses drove off.

Doctor Perkins followed them out, his taste for a drink forgotten. The horses did not take the direction of Seven Rivers. He stood in the shadows watching where they went and when he knew, he hurried back to the saloon.

Nothing of the tableau had changed. Sam still held Rob with his gun, not knowing how to move next. He could not simply walk away. Some frustrated Wertz would probably put a bullet in him for interfering. He decided that all he could do was back out of the room, taking Rob with him as a shield, and once outside, knock the boy cold and make a run for safety. Perkins' excited arrival spoiled that idea.

"They didn't leave town," the doctor said. "They left their horses behind the livery and broke into Tunny's gun shop for arms and ammunition. They'll be back here. Good night now." Perkins ducked out. This was no place to linger, and he knew he would be needed later.

Rob Wertz swore at Sam. "You sure raised hell. Take that damn gun off me, and let's get out of here where there's some room to fight."

"Truce," Sam said. "I'll fight with you. It's a different play."

He swung away toward the door, the men at the front turning that way. Sam pushed the louvered panels apart to see if Seven Rivers was in sight yet. A bullet from across the street bit into the jamb close to his head, and he dodged back, shouting for the overhead lamps to be doused.

The lights were shot out, leaving everyone in blinding dark. To his right the glass was broken out of a front window. He heard a scramble for the rear door, then rifle fire outside that, and knew his brother had men there too.

They were boxed inside. And if they stayed there Seven Rivers could be expected to burn the building, pick them off like clay pigeons escaping from the flames. For a moment Sam felt really trapped, then he remembered a way out from his boyhood. There had been a skylight over the pool table near the rear to give daylight to the players. The table was still there.

He called. "Bartender, is that skylight still in the roof?"

A shaky voice behind the counter said it was.

Holstering his gun Sam called again as he fumbled down the room. "Everybody to the pool table. I'll open the light and we can get to the roof. Be careful about noise."

He stumbled into moving figures, into the table, felt for a chair, and set it on the baize cover and climbed on that, feeling over his head. He touched the frame of the skylight, had to move the chair to be beneath the hole, then found the catch. It was rusted shut. Drawing the gun again he hammered with the butt. The catch was slow in giving. Sam hit it hard, and the tired metal broke. He could push the sash up but could not drag himself through it, high as it was above the chair.

Then Rob Wertz was on the table, his hands searching for Sam, following down his body to his legs, then lifting. Sam's arms locked over the frame and wriggling upward with Rob hoisting him higher, he rolled into the cool night air, kicked around, and reached down to pull on Wertz's hands.

16

One by one the men were pulled and pushed through the opening, rolling onto the roof, staying prone to present the lowest possible profile. There was no moon, but the stars cast an eerie sheen over the town.

Sam Allee crept around the roof looking for moving shadows on the ground. There was nothing to tell him where the Seven Rivers people were. The Wertz men lay along the four sides of the roof, Rob close beside Sam.

A torch flared in the alley across the street. Rob touched Sam's arm.

Sam whispered. "To fire the building. Pass the word, be ready to shoot when there's a target."

The warning went around the roof. The torch sputtered, catching enough to survive the throw, then was carried along the alley to the sidewalk. The man holding it stepped into sight, swinging his arm back for the cast. Sam Allee shot him.

They learned then where Drake's men were placed, on all sides of the saloon building. Guns winked toward the roof in a fusillade, tracking Sam's muzzle flash. Lead whistled over his head. There was a cry from one Wertz man as he was hit. They were firing back toward the ground, but there was no indication that the Seven Rivers people were struck.

Now each side knew where the other was, and it was imperative to get the clan's men down where there was shelter. It was only an eight-foot drop, but the sky was graying with coming dawn; there was light enough to make out a moving figure.

"Rob." He spoke softly and had a strained grunt in answer. "I'll go back through the skylight and start a diversion at the front. Hold your fire, and when they come after me get your boys off the roof quick. Make for the livery and the crew's horses."

A renewed volley made Sam hurry, but none of it came from the street or the buildings opposite the saloon. He dropped through the opening to the chair. It toppled, crashed to the floor, dumping him. Pain from his ribs lashed through him but he lit running, heading for the front window that had been broken out. Without caution he rolled over the sill, crouched for a second in the dark shade beside the wall, but no shot came. He sprinted, running low across the open street to the opposite sidewalk. The wooden awning hid him there.

The saddle shop beside the alley was dark, locked with an old-fashioned latch. Firing somewhere in the area erupted and under the sound Sam broke the latch with his gun butt. Inside the shop he felt a way along one wall, touching the bridles and harness hung against it on pegs, stumbling over saddles on the floor.

At the rear door he threw the bolt, eased the panel in, stretched his head out to look both ways. There was a man at either corner of the alley, behind the buildings, their rifles trained on the saloon roof, firing, then dodging back. Sam had only his short gun but it should carry the distance. He stepped outside, leveled the gun, steadied it with his left hand pressing his right against the wall, and squeezed off two shots. Both men yelled, spun around, fell. Sam was startled at how clearly he could see them, how much the light had grown.

He did not linger there. Before the echoes of his shots died he was running for the livery. There was sudden silence across the town. Seven Rivers was confused, not knowing where this new threat came from, afraid to shoot for fear of hitting one of their own. Sam hoped the Wertz men were using the respite to drop off the roof.

Behind the livery he found the horses tethered in a close group and stopped beside them, hidden in their bulk shadow. He stood catching his breath, listening, keen to locate any sound. It came shortly, a soft sighing, barely audible. Then they were there, Rob Wertz and his cousins, guns in one hand, shoes in the other, padding through the dust. Two were missing.

Stopping close in front of Sam, Rob whispered. "Know where Seven Rivers has got to?"

Sam shook his head, his breathing heavy.

Rob noted that. "You stay here and guard the horses while we look around town."

They were gone again, dropping the boots, sifting along the back of the buildings, disappearing like ghosts among the thinning shadows. A wooden water bucket lay in the dirt where it had been dropped rather than returned to the pump. Sam upended it and sat down. His ribs pulsed. His whole body ached. What he wanted most was rest, to stretch on the ground and sleep. But that must wait. To keep himself awake he reviewed the hours of the night.

It seemed to him that for the first time in his life he and his brother had come near some accord. But it was Martha Bollen, not Drake, who had created the illusion. Drake still resented him as he had Sam's mother. To Drake they were both interlopers, threats to the birthright Drake regarded as his alone. No, regardless of the eastern girl, Drake would never accept him. At best he would arrange some accident to Sam. The only solution must be to drive Drake from the Park.

Sam's attention was on the area behind the livery. He expected the Seven Rivers crew to come from that way for their horses, not through the barn from the street. He had no clear warning, only sensed that someone was near. He turned.

Drake Allee loomed in the broad doorway some dozen feet away, stopped in mid-stride, looking at Sam. Sam came to his feet slowly. As he rose his brother slapped toward his holster.

Sam spun. The move saved his life. Drake's gun exploded. A sudden burn stung Sam's left arm.

Even so his right hand dropped to his hip. His heavy weapon bucked twice as it swung up. Both slugs tore into Drake Allee's middle. He was driven back a step and stood swaying, trying with the last of his strength to aim his gun again. His hand would not obey. His knees buckled, dropped him, then the body collapsed on the hay-strewn runway floor.

Blood spilled down Sam's arm, left a trail of bright splotches as he walked forward. He did not holster his gun. The shots would bring the Seven Rivers crew. They too might be inside the barn. But no one fired from there.

He stood over his dead brother and knew that he looked down on a stranger and felt no remorse, only a dull anger that their lives could not have been otherwise.

Heavy breathing behind him made Sam jump, dodge into the dark shelter of a stall, raise his gun ready. But the running forms were Rob Wertz and three of his cousins, charging in without caution. Sam stepped into sight as they stopped at Drake's fallen body, saw the gun lying under the limp fingers. Rob raised his head, discovered the bloody rivulet down Sam's hanging left arm, and blew a gusty breath.

"That close? Well, this ends it all. We cornered the crew when they tried for our horses at the saloon. They're corralled inside under guard."

Sam said tiredly, "You still set on hanging them?"

Rob shrugged. "With Drake gone they don't matter. I'm glad you stopped us before. Bad thing to live with afterward. We'll run them off later. First let's have that arm patched before you leak out all your blood."

The new day shimmered pale in the street as Rob Wertz steadied Sam Allee's wobbly steps out of the barn. Sam insisted that before he saw the doctor he was going to visit Emily Pease's house to learn how Milly was, and Rob did not argue against that. The windows glowed with light upstairs and down. The door stood open.

Rob hurried Allee up to the porch, leaving the cousins on the walk, crowding into the front room, saying anxiously, "What's wrong? Is it Milly?"

Perkins sagged on the sofa, his hands clasped between his knees, looking exhausted. Martha Bollen sat at the table, her arms still and limp on the paisley cover, her face pale and empty. Sam Allee's heart stopped. Milly had died.

The doctor raised his head. "It isn't Milly. Milly's fine. It's the crop of cases that piled in here. You bringing more?" Sam was already on his way to the closed bedroom door when the doctor's order stopped him. "Stay out of there, Sam. She's conscious but I put her to sleep, sedated her. She's worn out. Hell, what a night. She was bound and determined to get up and go chasing around looking for you two when she heard what was going on. All the shooting."

Perkins' busy eyes had settled on Sam Allee's bloody sleeve. He stood up, moving wearily, to examine the wound. Martha Bollen saw the sleeve too and got to her feet, leaning against the table for support, then dropped back when Perkins spoke.

"Sit down, this don't need you." To Sam and Rob he added, "She's watched over Milly most of the night, and the rest she spent with me and Emily mending damn fools. The house is full of them. How long is this idiocy going on?"

Relief that Milly was alive, would recover,

washed through Sam Allee, followed by an exultant elation at her show of caring; then reaction set in. He sank onto the chair opposite Martha Bollen.

"No longer," he answered Perkins.

"Drake?"

Sam closed his eyes. He hated to go on with the girl listening, but she would hear it sometime and maybe this was the best, with other people present.

He said dully; "Dead. He tried to kill me." He moved the left arm. "I shot back." To the white-faced blonde he softened his tone. "I'm sorry, Martha. There's money enough now to send you east, help you. I can't ask you to marry me now."

Oddly, Sam thought, a sardonic smile pulled her lips to one side and her chin lifted. She looked defiant. "I know. Milly. I heard her. I see you, how it is. It's best for me too this way. I didn't love you anyway, and I don't need your help."

Perkins was working on the arm, had swabbed it with antiseptic that made Sam wince, then painted it with procaine. Sam ignored him, caught by something like laughter in Martha Bollen's tone.

"That five hundred won't take you far." He sounded puzzled.

"It won't have to. I didn't tell you before because there was no reason to. When Drake courted me in St. Louis, he used a tempting bait. Made a will leaving Seven Rivers to me even if he died before we were married. It's a valid will. I own the ranch now."

Perkins plunged the suture needle deeper than he meant to, into the unanesthetized flesh, as shocked as Sam by the girl's disclosure. Sam swore, more at the words than the pain, his heart sinking. Even in death his brother could rob him. His eyes held sick on her face.

Then she laughed aloud. "I couldn't run it, of course. You'll have to do that. Will you? Run it on shares, cattle for each of us? And you keep the Allen place for your own? So I can go home where I belong?"

Sam Allee's mouth opened slowly, then his grin came, full and strong. He nodded. Perkins jabbed the needle in again. The pain was beautiful, searing Sam back to reality. For the first time in his life he knew total happiness.

John Hunter was the name used by **Todhunter Ballard** for a number of outstanding Western novels. Ballard was born in Cleveland, Ohio. He graduated with a Bachelor's degree from Wilmington College in Ohio, having majored in mechanical engineering. His early years were spent working as an engineer before he began writing fiction for the magazine market. As W. T. Ballard he was one of the regular contributors to *Black Mask Magazine* along with Dashiell Hammett and Erle Stanley Gardner. Although Ballard published his first Western story in *Cowboy Stories* in 1936, the same year he married Phoebe Dwiggins, it wasn't until *Two-Edged Vengeance* (1951) that he produced his first Western novel. Ballard later claimed that Phoebe, following their marriage, had co-written most of his fiction with him, and perhaps this explains, in part, his memorable female characters. Ballard's Golden Age as a Western author came in the 1950s and extended to the early 1970s. *Incident at Sun Mountain* (1952), *West of Quarantine* (1953), and *High Iron* (1953) are among his finest early historical titles, published by Houghton Mifflin. After numerous traditional Westerns for various publishers, Ballard returned to the historical novel in *Gold in California!* (1965) which earned him a Golden Spur Award from the Western Writers of America. It is a story set during the Gold Rush era of the 'Forty-Niners. However, an even more panoramic view of that same era is to be found in Ballard's *magnum opus, The Californian* (1971), with its contrasts between the *Californios* and the emigrant gold-seekers, and the building of a freight line to compete with Wells Fargo. It was in his historical fiction that Ballard made full use of his background in engineering combined with exhaustive historical research. However, these novels are also character-driven, gripping a reader from first page to last with their inherent drama and the spirit of adventure so true of those times.